A MAN'S WORD

Also available in The King's Hounds series

The King's Hounds
Oathbreaker

MARTIN JENSEN

A MAN'S WORD

Translated by Tara F. Chace

amazoncrossing

Text copyright © 2012 by Martin Jensen and Forlaget Klim

English translation copyright © 2015 by Tara F. Chace

Printed in the United States of America.

A Man's Word was first published as *En bondes ord* by Klim in 2012. Translated from the Danish by Tara F. Chace. Published in English by AmazonCrossing in 2014.

Published by AmazonCrossing, Seattle

ISBN-13: 9781477822203
ISBN-10: 1477822208
LCCN: 2014916474

Cover design by Edward Bettison
Front cover pitchfork illustration created by Edward Bettison

Floral pattern from The Art of Illumination, Dover Pictura, 2009, royalty-free

Back cover illustration public domain images found in the British Library Catalogue of Illuminated Manuscripts, http://www.bl.uk/catalogues /illuminatedmanuscripts/reuse.asp

England, Anno Domini 1018

SCOTLAND

NORTH SEA

NORTHUMBRIA

IRISH SEA

THE DANELAW

IRELAND

PETERBOROUGH

DANES' FORD

MERCIA ENGLAND

EAST ANGLIA
THETFORD
EDMUND'S TOWN

WALES

WATLING STREET

OXFORD

LONDON

WESSEX

The Hundred Court

1

Eadred shot the arrow into its target without hesitating. The monastery's sharpshooter was the best archer I had ever met. He could sight down the shaft past the arrowhead, even at a target in motion, and hit the mark practically every time.

The goose stopped midflight, struck by the heavy fowl-hunting arrow. It folded its wings and fell, spinning down after the arrow, which struck the surface of the water a second before the dead bird. They had scarcely hit the lake before Eadred's muffled whistle dispatched his long-legged dog to splash out into the water and return with both the bird and the arrow in his mouth.

I gave the archer an appreciative smile. Then I stretched and breathed the fresh spring air deep into my lungs, while my gaze followed a skein of squawking barnacle geese on their way north after a night's rest in the marsh.

Eadred and I had become friends over the winter. I'd saved him from a nasty beating in an alehouse, where he'd flirted with the wrong wench.

The evening Eadred and I met, just before Christmas, I was sitting peacefully over a tankard of ale after spending yet another idle day wandering through the town. At the town's center was the monastery where my master, Winston, spent his days meticulously filling pages of parchment with illustrations in accordance with an agreement he'd made with the monks.

We lived in one of the buildings the monks owned, a post-and-plank structure outside the monastery itself. "We" included me, Winston, and his woman, Alfilda. Alfilda had sold her tavern in Oxford to shack up with my master and follow him wherever his text-illuminating expertise took him.

In the mornings when I emerged from my own chamber, she had already set out warm ale and porridge for us. Winston and I would sit on either side of the plank table, and once she was sure we had enough in our bowls, she would sit down beside Winston.

I usually left with my master in the morning, parting from him at the entrance to the monastery. Then, I was on my own for the rest of the day. By the time I came home shortly before dark, Alfilda would have seen to our supper, so her days were probably filled with visits to market stalls and little shops. At any rate, the meals were quite ample as well as expertly prepared.

Now and then Prior Edmund would send a messenger to fetch me, and I would gladly comply; these occasions meant a welcome break from my idleness.

Once he wanted me to take a message to the Archbishop of York—a trip I was particularly glad to make since it entailed three whole weeks of riding through the countryside. Other times his desires were more modest: Would I accompany a noble guest to the next resting place or inn? Would I ride out with the monastery's spearmen to collect taxes from the villages on the monastery's property? But no matter how great or small the task was, I would agree to it—not out of love for those monastic farts but for the chance to break out of my rut.

So one evening just before Christmas, after a day devoid of any challenges greater than remembering suppertime, I left Winston and Alfilda as soon as I had gulped down the last of my lard-slathered bread and headed to the alehouse, where I hoped to run into a certain redheaded lass who had previously agreed to spend the night with me.

She never showed up, and the other wenches, who giggled to each other and flashed their gums in flirtatious grins, did not entice me. So I was sitting quietly in my seat against the wall—I always like to have an unimpeded view of any establishment I find myself in—enjoying the tang of the sweet-gale-flavored ale when the door opened.

The girl who walked in was somewhat more inviting than the other whores, and the way she conducted herself quickly convinced me she did not share their profession. All the same, I refrained from going over to her since I still hoped the redheaded wench might show up.

A thin man dressed in a peasant's coat did decide to approach her. I recognized him as the monastery's archer from the few times we'd run into each other in the chapter house.

His name was Eadred, as I later learned. He immediately sat down beside the wench and started gabbing away. Even though she apparently turned down his offer of a drink, she still seemed to listen to him, although I did notice her eyes straying over to the door at regular intervals.

I had just emptied my tankard when the door swung open again, revealing three young men. They headed straight for Eadred's table, where he had just made the girl laugh about something.

They were solid-looking boys, those three. They had broad shoulders and chests, with upper arms like my thighs, and they strode purposefully across the packed-dirt floor to the table, where the girl was the first to notice them. She smiled at the boy in front, a Saxon with flaxen braids hanging down his back. She offered him her hand with a gesture more suitable for a relative than a lover.

Eadred leaned back and stared into space, apparently too wise to provoke three strangers by looking them in the eye. All the same, one of the other two stepped forward and leaned menacingly over the table. Only those seated nearby could hear what he said to the archer, but Eadred's flush of anger and pursed lips gave me a good idea.

I watched the archer rise with an exaggerated slowness, making it clear that like everyone else in the tavern, he was armed. Then he calmly walked across the room.

I was convinced he had yielded not because of fear, but because he knew he would get the worst of it if it came to blows with the three boys. In addition, he was the monastery's archer and subject to the abbot's rules. No one in the service of the abbot was allowed to get into fights.

Maybe everything would have gone better if he hadn't turned around after a few steps to nod farewell to the girl. It was an innocent gesture that nonetheless provoked the three rascals, who didn't hesitate to step forward and grab hold of him.

My assumption that his retreat was not due to fear of a brawl proved correct, because as soon as he freed himself from their grasp, his hands were up and ready to fight.

The boys closed in on him right away. The one in front took a swing at the archer's jaw. Eadred dodged him while hammering his own right hand into his attacker's breastbone. The guy faltered but managed to stay afoot, and with a muffled oath, the first boy who had spoken to Eadred launched forward to punch Eadred in the gut.

I briefly contemplated whether this fight was any of my business, but of course I knew I couldn't just stand by as a passive observer and let one of the monastery's men be beaten to a pulp just for speaking to an attractive wench. So I reached across my table, grabbed the tankard of the man sitting closest to me, and jettisoned its contents into the attackers' faces. Then I followed up by smashing the tankard itself into the back of the closest attacker's skull. That one collapsed to the ground with a hollow cough.

The other two looked around in confusion, a blunder that allowed Eadred and me to each fell a man, after which we stepped outside and strolled away down the street shoulder to shoulder, without saying a word.

That was the beginning of our friendship, which was further solidified when I entered the chapter house the next day to testify about the incident in the pub. Those three gamecocks had accused Eadred of assaulting them. I testified that this charge was baseless and that, to the contrary, it was they who had attacked Eadred, who had conducted himself as a perfect monastery layman in every regard.

Eadred's friendship had made my days far less plodding. I often rode out hunting with him. I never did learn to be as good a shot with a bow and arrow as he was, but I was better at letting wild boars skewer themselves to death on my spear. As a former soldier, I understood how to position the spear correctly so that the brunt of the boar's strength flowed through the length of the spear instead of trying to counter the attacking animal's weight, which would splinter the shaft.

The archer was rarely idle, for the monks—who themselves lived by the Rule of Saint Benedict and didn't eat the flesh of four-footed animals—were generous with their guests and gladly set out venison steaks and boar alongside roast beef and ham on the guests' table. I went hunting with him whenever I could.

On this drizzly spring morning, we'd ridden north into the fens that extend from a few miles west of the monastery all the way to Thetford in the east, then gradually disappear in the south as you move through East Anglia into Essex, and end in the north at the Wash, the bay that juts into the land from the North Sea.

The marshland was hard to move around in if you weren't from there, but I felt like I was in good hands since Eadred had grown up in a small town in the middle of a local polder, low-lying marshland he claimed the Romans had reclaimed with dikes. He knew every path, every half-eroded dike, every age-old cobblestone, and he guided me safely. With Eadred in the lead, we rode through the drizzle, which gradually gave way to spring sunshine so that half a dozen geese hung from each of our saddles by the sun's midday zenith. The geese were destined for the abbot's end-of-fast table tomorrow, as the abbot had decided on some roast goose to please his palate.

We rested on a little knoll, scarcely bigger than a tussock, and wolfed down a couple thick slabs of bread and allowed ourselves a taste of the ale from the cask. Then we slowly walked the horses back to the monastery.

The day was bright and fresh, and countless birds flew over us on their way north. The sun warmed our tunics, and deep down I hoped restlessness would soon uproot my master from Peterborough; the spring made the idea of moving on most inviting.

But Winston hadn't seemed inclined to move on. He had been idle for a few weeks now that he had completed a large book about Seaxwulf for the monastery. Lord knows the monks had paid him well, and he, Alfilda, and I did not want for anything. To the contrary, we had enough to last for a long time. And we had more than just the money from Winston's illuminations, for King Cnut had given us a handsome reward for a little job we'd done for him on our way to Peterborough.

Winston seemed satisfied to idle away his days with Alfilda. Every time I suggested we move on, he would just shake his head and mumble that Peterborough was as fine a place to let the days slip by as anywhere else.

I led the horses to the monastery stable while Eadred delivered our fowl to the cook. Our plan was to reunite and then pay a visit to the nearest tavern, but a novice grabbed me to say my master had been asking for me.

"Winston the Illuminator?" I was surprised Winston had even left the building we were staying in.

The novice nodded and said, "He was in the chapter house a while ago."

I told Eadred he'd have to drink his ale alone, and I headed home through the narrow town streets to our quarters.

Winston and Alfilda were both sitting at the table when I walked in. Alfilda turned to me and smiled while Winston made do with just looking up.

"So you're back," he said sarcastically.

Which was downright childish. He knew I'd been out hunting and had no instructions to hurry back. Still, I just nodded because I noticed the letter on the table between them.

"Well, there is the end to your life of ease," Winston said, tipping his head at the letter.

I didn't say anything. I figured he was annoyed to be uprooted from our current situation, although surely, like me, he realized it was only a question of time before the monks kicked us out.

"We're heading southeast," he said, like a peevish child.

I flashed him an encouraging smile and said, "Southeast, huh? Into East Anglia? I've never been there. Is the letter from the king?"

He nodded and held the letter out toward me, but then set it back down when he remembered that reading was not a skill I had mastered.

"It's from Cnut, yes. It was delivered by a soldier, who rode back right away. The king is in Hampton."

Presumably with his consort, Ælfgifu, and her son. More importantly, Hampton was only a day's ride from Peterborough. The soldier must have set out that same morning, and the king would receive confirmation of the delivery by nightfall.

"So what will we be doing among the East Anglians?" I asked, taking a seat across from Winston and Alfilda.

"Humph," Winston said, smoothing out the letter, his eyes following the spidery signs running across it in even lines. "Cnut has asked me to go to Saint Edmund's church and offer my artistry to the monks there."

Saint Edmund is said to have defeated Cnut's father, Sweyn Forkbeard, with a deadly disease when Sweyn threatened to burn the church and the whole town unless he received the taxes he demanded.

I smiled at Winston. "So the king wants to suck up to the saint who killed his father."

Winston smiled wryly back and said, "That's what the monks are meant to believe."

I had already guessed the king was not dispatching us out of piety. I pondered his real motivation, which wasn't easy with Winston looking at me with a teasing smirk on his face. He obviously already knew the answer to my unspoken question; the king's messenger had likely just told him. But I figured it out quickly on my own anyway.

"Thorkell," I said.

Winston nodded. "Jarl Thorkell, formerly Cnut's and his father's most powerful enemy and now his sworn man, yes."

This wasn't the first time we'd run up against Cnut's—justifiable—mistrust of his jarls. The king used men like Winston and me, who could move through the land surreptitiously, to safeguard himself against seditious, rebellious noblemen who sought to throw the country into war.

"Let's hear it," I said, leaning over the table.

Not that there was much to hear. The king's message as relayed by his housecarl went like this: "Head into East Anglia, and be my eyes and ears."

Despite its brevity, the implication was clear. The only reason to send us to East Anglia was to sniff out what we could about Jarl Thorkell. People called him Thorkell the Tall, and not without reason. He was not only taller than most men, but he also had a very lofty view of himself. He had already changed sides a number of times.

I once heard him called Thorkell Turncoat by a man who didn't live long after he called him that.

2

efore we sat down to supper, we decided we might as well set off the next day. Actually, *Winston* decided. I looked at him in puzzlement because past experience had shown that he needed at least a day to pack up his paints, brushes, jars, and paper cones—all of the equipment he needed to do his illuminations.

It turned out he had packed it all up the previous week, that sly old fox. In other words, even if he wasn't quite as eager to move on as I was, he hadn't been planning on staying at the monastery forever.

The only hard part, then, was deciding which road to take. The best sniffing is generally not done on the shortest route. We agreed on that.

So we had two options. The first was to stick to a western route as we rode south, skirting the large Bruneswald forest and making our way through the fens to the Cam Bridge, and from there heading northeastward to our final destination. However, that route would take us along the eastern border of Mercia, keeping us out of East Anglia until the end. It didn't make sense, since our job was to spend as much time as possible in Thorkell's jarldom in East Anglia.

We quickly chose the second option of traveling due east through the fens, crossing the River Ouse at the place that goes by the name of Danes' Ford, and continuing out of the marsh until we reached the Icknield Way. We could then travel south through Thetford until we reached the track that ran east to Saint Edmund's Town.

Two things supported this option: We would be moving through the jarl's area as soon as we'd left Peterborough, and we would have the opportunity to linger in Thetford, the most important town in East Anglia and therefore the best place to sniff out gossip and talk.

Once we agreed on this, I left Winston and Alfilda to finish the packing while I went to find Eadred.

Eadred lived at the edge of a cluster of houses constituting the monastery's outbuildings, in a cottage with his blind father, who had been an archer before him but had lost his vision at the Battle of Maldon, where he fought with Byrhtnoth.

Eadred invited me right in, offering me a seat in the cottage's single, smoke-filled room. His father's bench was positioned right in front of the hearth, while Eadred's own was pushed all the way back against the opposite wall. We sat down on Eadred's bench while his father laboriously sat up from under his blankets, cleared his throat, and made a wet chuckle as he accepted the tankard of ale his son thrust into his hand.

They both listened to my news, said they were sorry I had to leave—the old man enjoyed my visits since I would let him blabber on about the old days and moral decline—and assured me their words would guide me as safely through the fens as if they were leading me on their own horses.

Although Eadred did most of the talking, the old man interjected his opinions at regular intervals. And even though the old man hadn't been out in the fens for years, it was clear to me his blind eyes nonetheless hid a kind of vision that would stay with him until the day he died.

"The first bit of the way is easy enough," Eadred began. "You just follow the old paved road the Romans built many years ago. Of course it's always possible winter changed things a little, but since there wasn't much frost, it's not likely. You should be able to ride as far as the River Nene without problems, because the stones in the road are well maintained that far."

The old man cleared his throat, spat on the floor, and said, "The ford is marked with a red cross."

"No," Eadred said, shaking his head. "The ford has moved further north now. You'll find a cairn about forty paces north of the stone bridge."

"On the other side of the river, the pavement is missing," the old man said, seeming irritated at having been corrected.

His son gave me a wry smile.

"That's right, Father. It's completely gone for the first five or ten miles, but the track isn't hard to follow since poles have been set out. Just remember to keep them on your left."

"Otherwise you'll get your feet wet," the old man teased.

"Wet feet? They'll get water up to the saddle at this time of year," Eadred said. "Then you'll come to the paving again and follow that all the way to the Danes' Ford."

"And the ford is not actually marked there," the old man said, holding out his tankard.

Eadred got up and filled it from the cask, which was covered by a wet cloth.

"There are a few huts and the folks living there will show you the ford for a gratuity," Eadred said.

"Which shouldn't be big." The old man raised his left hand to me. "In the old days, people helped travelers out by marking the ford."

Eadred nodded in agreement. "But the ford moves because of the current, so now the people who live there keep an eye on it and accept payment for guiding travelers across."

"Too bad those Viking bandits were able to find it when they came." The old man spat on the floor again. "Otherwise I'd still be able to enjoy the sight of a beautiful woman."

"On the far side of the Ouse the paved sections come and go. You should pay attention and always stop if you notice the cobblestones under your feet are gone. Ride half an arrowshot apart so you can use each other to maintain a line of sight. The track runs straight ahead, so if you keep in a line the whole time, you can't get lost."

"Yes, that's how it is all the way to the Icknield Way," the father said, hawking up a clot of mucus and then rinsing it down with ale.

"Are you clear on how to go now?" Eadred asked me.

I closed my eyes halfway, thought back over it, and then repeated the instructions they'd given me. Eadred nodded and refilled the tankards again. We emptied them while chatting. At one point, Eadred suddenly gave me a stern look and asked *why* I was going to be sure to keep the poles to my right.

I thought for a moment and then said, "Because . . . because otherwise we'll sink into the marsh." Obviously.

"You certainly will. Especially if you don't pay better attention."

I stared at him blankly, but then I realized: "On my left! You said to keep them on my left."

Then he went through it all once more. And then after yet another tankard, one final time.

The old man had fallen asleep now, but Eadred and I chatted for another while before I left. Eadred walked out with me, and after we'd both peed on a fence, he asked me to run through his instructions again. Which I did to his satisfaction. Then we parted ways.

When Winston and I rode north on the king's business last fall, it was on horses from Cnut's stables. Once we reached Peterborough, no one knew exactly whose horses they were, so they spent the winter alongside Winston's malevolent mule, Atheling, and Winston had paid the monastery for the care of all three.

I fetched them in the morning as though it were the most natural thing in the world and saddled first my master's gray mare, then my own red gelding, while Winston struggled to get all the parcels stowed and secured on Atheling's back, a job encumbered by the annoyance the old nag felt at being forced to work.

Alfilda saddled her own woolly mare, which had brought her north after she sold her tavern, made sure that her own clothes as well as her lover's were cinched on behind the saddles, and then took up position. She smiled as she watched Winston, who was struggling, red-faced with anger, to keep his mule still so that the last small packages could be secured to its back.

I fastened my own pack to the gelding's saddle, made sure my sword sheath was nice and secure under the saddle's left thigh roll, the hilt sticking out forward so that I could easily draw the weapon if necessary.

Winston bade the abbot and prior farewell immediately after breakfast while I packed up my things. Knowing Winston, I presumed it hadn't been a tearful good-bye since the monks were surely just as happy to see us go now that Winston's work was done.

"You could give me a hand," Winston said with a scowl. He was now drenched in sweat after his struggles with Atheling.

"I could." I nodded. "But you know how well your damned animal and I get along. The second Atheling sees me, he chomps at my shoulder as though it were a tuft of hay."

Winston looked angry, but he didn't say anything. On our various journeys together I had tried in vain to convince him that Atheling was a devilish beast that seized any opportunity to bite, kick, or butt me with his head. Winston would always respond that it was just me, that I didn't know how to manage the animal properly.

When he was finally done, he tightened the last cord and glanced from Alfilda to me.

"We should probably be under way," he said.

I took up the lead, followed by Alfilda. We then slowly rode past the monastery while Winston tried to follow, leading Atheling by hand. I could tell from Winston's cursing that that old hack of a mule was resisting the tug of the rope, so I turned around in my saddle to ask him if he needed help. Winston's mare, eager to get going after the long winter, was circling the mule, which had sat down on its haunches. The lead between Winston's hand and Atheling's halter was taut.

Alfilda turned her mare around before I even had a chance to ask. With a determined look on her face, she circled back around behind Winston and Atheling, pulled her mare up next to the seated mule and stopped. She pulled her feet out of her stirrups, leaned over to the right and gave the mule a swift and solid kick with enough strength that Atheling got up again with a whiny bray.

Alfilda kicked Atheling again, and the still-grumbling beast surged forward so quickly it passed Winston, who nearly dropped the lead in surprise. But at the last second, Winston dug his heels into his own mare and caught up to the mule in two strides. They passed me and my gelding before I got him going again.

All in all, a memorable departure from the monastery.

3

It wasn't hard to follow the instructions Eadred and his father had given me. The spring sun was shining, so it was a pleasant ride to the River Nene, although we were only able to move at a walk since the pavement had suffered in the many years since the Romans had built the road.

We rested on a hillock that jutted up a couple feet above the marsh. Even this slight elevation was enough to give us a view over the vast, flat fens. Geese and ducks flew overhead and a yellowhammer sang annoyingly from a bush as the nags grazed and we shared a loaf of bread and some dry cheese from the monastery's stores, and a nice cask of ale.

After the meal we rested a bit more and then resumed our ride to the east. We did not see any travelers, save one—a solitary priest riding toward us on a hinny, his head lolling. He greeted us and, without any encouragement, shared that he was on his way from the cathedral in Elmham with a message for the abbey in Ramsey. It turned out he'd never ridden this way before, and he inquired anxiously about the condition of the road. Then he calmly proceeded toward Peterborough, where we had assured him he could find a guide who would take him the rest of the way through the marshland.

Aside from him, we had the road to ourselves all the way to the river.

There were no villages or farms out here in the flooded fens, so the rumble of ox-drawn wagons one otherwise encountered when traveling was absent. I learned from Winston, who knows this kind of thing, that the Romans had built this road to ensure their soldiers a quick march to engage the Iceni, who, led by their queen, were trying to throw off the Roman yoke. Since then the road had borne Saxons and Angles, and then Danish overlords, each tromping their way in turn through the countryside to attack Mercia's eastern border.

We reached the ford over the Nene later that evening and decided to cross before it got dark. We easily found the spot Eadred had described, but as we started into the river I realized that fords sometimes move, and I bitterly cursed the clergyman we had run into earlier for not describing the ford's current position to us.

Luckily I had ridden out first, and Winston's mare hadn't even gotten her pasterns wet before I turned my gelding around because water was pouring over his back. Alfilda's horse wasn't in over the knees yet and walked willingly back to the shore, where Alfilda and Winston waited as I rode up and down the river looking for a place to cross.

I finally found it half an arrowshot farther north than the ford, and all three of us managed to cross before it was completely dark.

We found a dry area a ways up the bluff and spread our blankets in the grass, but there were no trees or dry cow dung we could use as fuel, so we shared another loaf of bread along with some salted leg of lamb. As we ate, we huddled together under the various blankets we'd brought for the horses and ourselves.

Winston thought I should go back across the river to move the cairn, but I refused. It was dark, and I didn't think it would do any good since we couldn't know when the ford would move again. Instead we agreed that we would make anyone we ran into the following evening at Danes' Ford, or Dena Fær as it was known locally, aware of the crossing so that they could send word to Peterborough and have the cairn moved.

The night passed without problems, aside from a rumbling I recognized as Winston's snoring. I lay awake for a while struggling to block the sound from my ears with the blankets.

When I grumpily asked Alfilda the next morning how she could sleep next to her thunder-breathing paramour, she grinned and showed me two small tufts of wool. She confided in a whisper that the last thing she always did before going to sleep was to stuff them in her ears.

Although the paving stones were missing on this side of the river, we still made good time since the track was very clearly marked by poles, which I remembered to keep on my left. After a midday rest, the pavement started again, and now it was in even better shape than the first stretch, so we reached Danes' Ford late in the afternoon.

We came to a cluster of cottages surrounded by fish-drying racks, and flat-bottomed punts pulled up onto the grass. A fellow with a black beard and a gravelly voice met us and offered us shelter for the night, if we wanted. Otherwise he would take us across the River Ouse for a small sum.

We accepted his offer of shelter. After a meal of smoked goose breast, salted eel, and sour rye bread, Winston and Alfilda found space in one of the cottages. I preferred to sleep out under the open sky to keep my ears on our animals—and as far away from Winston's snoring as possible.

In the morning, Black Beard led us across the river, and it wasn't until I looked back from the bluff that I saw silhouettes around the huts, including a wench with her skirt tucked up, with whom I would have enjoyed becoming acquainted the night before. But I assumed villagers had learned from experience to keep everyone beside Black Beard away when there were travelers at the ford, and I was sure that the men had slept with their swords at the ready.

On the third day, I remembered Eadred's advice to ride single file, and I sent Alfilda and Winston on ahead with instructions to ride with half an arrowshot between them and to listen for my shouts from behind.

Just as Eadred had said, the pavement sometimes disappeared from beneath our horses. Each time it did, I used my companions to form a line of sight. We made slower progress than on the previous days, but nonetheless we starting climbing out of the fens by late morning. We took our midday meal at the place where the Fen Causeway crossed the Icknield Way.

We had left the fens behind us—looking back, we now had an unimpeded view of their vast expanse—and had reached the most important track leading south through the land of the North Folk, the rest of East Anglia, and into Mercia.

There were more travelers now. Peddlers struggled along under the weight of their wares; merchants sat atop donkey tumbrels or wagons, which creaked along; now and again mounted soldiers came rushing out of nowhere and forced everyone to make way; and a few farmers drove their flocks toward the waiting market.

After we wiped the lamb fat from our mouths, we saddled up again, and turned our animals southward, riding just off the road to bypass slow-moving travelers. By midafternoon we reached the sandy inland, which had loomed above us since we'd left the low-lying fens.

We had to cross a small river here, too deep for us to ford unless we wanted to move a few miles to the west, so a freckled boy ferried us across instead. He studied the coin Winston placed in his hand for a long time and then spit on it before sliding it into the leather pouch that hung around his neck.

When we asked whether there was any shelter before we reached Thetford, he only shrugged and then spit again, although this time into the river. It wasn't until our horses had set their hooves on solid ground that he mumbled only fools traversed the heath in the dark.

Luckily we found a little hamlet south of the river. Not much to look at, but big enough to contain three farms, two medium in size and one so large that its farmhouse was more of a small hall, a typical one-room dwelling with a hearth in the middle of the floor, whose residents would eat and sleep communally. It was surprisingly large given the size of the hamlet.

Winston had been in front since we reached the Icknield Way, and he now led us to the hall. He left me holding both Atheling's and his mare's reins, pounded on the door with his fist to announce his arrival, and then ducked to enter.

Alfilda slid down from her saddle, rubbing her lower back, but her eyes were trained on a kite soaring overhead and scanning for carrion.

I suddenly noticed a pretty young woman emerging from a path between the farms. Her blonde braids hung over her breasts, which swelled beneath the freshly laundered gray blouse. Her skirt and bare feet signaled she was a slave. She walked tall and looked me in the eye without averting her gaze.

I waved to her and wanted to say hello, but she continued past me without a sideways glance, disappearing into the hall just as Winston came out.

"We're welcome to spend the night here," he reported, holding his hand out to Alfilda, who took it and accompanied him back inside while I led our animals into a wickerwork paddock I had discovered kitty-corner behind the hall.

I managed to get the saddles off and brought our things under the cover of a lean-to, all while successfully avoiding Atheling's attempts to bite me. I thwacked him on the forehead to tell him to behave and led him into the paddock last. He immediately headed over to a frightened-looking filly, who told him with a well-aimed kick to stay over by the far fence.

A fire roared upon the hearthstones in the middle of the one-room hall. Thick weavings hung on the walls, and the man my companions were talking to seemed self-confident and yet accommodating as Winston introduced us.

"This is Arnulf, whose bread we have been invited to break," Winston said.

I could hear from his tone that we should treat the man with respect, so I bowed and gave his outstretched hand a firm squeeze.

We were immediately invited to take a seat on the bench that ran along the wall. Arnulf sat down in a chair with no armrests but with a woven seat and backrest. Not just a high seat, I thought, as I gratefully accepted a tankard of ale from the slave girl. I winked at her, but she'd already turned her back to me, so I contented myself by draining half the tankard—no hardship considering the strongly malted, tasty drink.

Winston and our host spoke quietly while I looked around the hall. I could make out several figures as my eyes adjusted. In the cooking area, the stout mistress was barking orders to three or four girls. A couple of boys sat on the floor nearby, carving spoons or wooden shoes—I couldn't see which—and three slaves carried out a plank that they set on a couple of trestles in front of the hearth, close enough that the fire would still warm those who sat there, but far enough away that they wouldn't roast.

My eyes came to rest on our host. He was about thirty, my height but a little burlier, with broad shoulders. His blond hair was neatly trimmed, his clothes clean and well made, and his freshly trimmed Saxon mustache hung down around his mouth.

My eyes scanned in vain for the sword that should have been leaning against his chair, and when I glanced at the bed behind the trestle table, I saw no weapon there either. Nor could I hear or spot the dogs that are permanent fixtures in every thane's hall.

The explanation came during the meal, which was copious and well prepared. Alfilda was invited to enjoy the food, even though the lady of the house remained in the kitchen area. Arnulf explained that we could travel together the next day since he had business in Thetford. "Partly," he said, chewing a crust of bread, "because the market tomorrow is open to all farmers."

I sensed Winston looking at me and nodded to show that I, too, had understood that we were not the guests of a thane here but rather of a ceorl, a well-to-do farmer.

Winston politely waited for Arnulf to finish chewing before he asked, "Partly?"

Our host nodded and said, "The Hundred Court is sitting in Thetford the day after tomorrow, and I have a case against a man."

We looked at him with curiosity as he sat wearing the serious expression men adopt when they want their audience's full attention.

Arnulf was in no rush and raised his tankard to drink to us. I had already emptied mine, but the slave wench appeared in a flash, refilling it with one hand, which shook at the exertion of managing the heavy pitcher.

The farmer set his tankard down.

Winston asked if the case had anything to do with land. "Or perhaps an inheritance?"

Arnulf shook his head meaningfully. "No, it's about a rape."

4

lfilda, Winston, and I looked at one another in surprise.

A ceorl like Arnulf would not typically put up with the rape of a relative long enough to take it to court. He would gather his kinsmen and friends to exact revenge, allowing a spearhead to do the talking.

But our host sat before us utterly calm, apparently content with the situation, or at least with our astonished looks.

Winston finished chewing his mouthful. "Rape?" he asked quietly, surveying the hall.

My gaze also swept through the room without spotting any women other than the ones, like the wench, who were flocking around the mistress of the house in the kitchen area.

Arnulf nodded and brought a piece of meat to his mouth with the tip of his knife.

"And the victim?" I asked.

"That wench there," Arnulf said, gesturing with his hand.

We looked where he was pointing. Ah, so the girl's hands weren't trembling from the weight of the ale pitcher but from dread that her shame would be put on display.

Winston kept his eyes on our host, but Alfilda and I exchanged meaningful glances: if that was Arnulf's daughter, he must be really stingy not to dress her the way a farmer's daughter should be dressed. I felt a vague discomfort at this stinginess, leaving a freeborn girl to walk around in slave's rags.

"Your slave?" asked Winston, who apparently was not thinking the same thing.

Our host belched behind his hand, and leaned back in his chair. "Yes, my slave wench. I had been hoping to fetch a good price for her."

Alfilda seemed displeased, but I nodded knowingly at the farmer's words. A slender, pretty slave wench would have fetched significantly more if she went to her new master unsullied.

"So you must have sought compensation in vain," Winston concluded, sitting very still, but I saw his jaw muscles tremble slightly.

"And why would you suppose that?" Arnulf said in surprise.

"Why?" Winston echoed with a shrug. "You're a man who values affluence, if I'm not mistaken."

"What's your point?" Arnulf asked, narrowing his eyes.

"Well, you must have sought compensation for your loss," Winston replied. "In vain, I presume, because otherwise there would be no reason to take your case to the Hundred Court."

Arnulf bit his lip and nodded.

"The culprit didn't think he had committed a crime, then?" Winston asked, rubbing his chin.

Arnulf's response was a snort.

"Well, at any rate, he refused to reimburse you?" Winston surmised. Only Alfilda and I could recognize the contempt in Winston's voice, his disdain for a man who valued money more than anything else in life.

Alfilda leaned over the table and asked, "Perhaps we could hear the whole story?"

Arnulf ignored her and held his tankard out to the slave wench, who filled it immediately.

"What my woman means," Winston said, his jaw muscles working hard now to conceal his rage, "is that it would be easier for us to understand the whole thing if we knew the background."

"It's none of your business," Arnulf said, shaking his head.

"Quite true," Winston admitted, shooting Alfilda a glance that silenced her. "But apparently you wanted us to be aware of it."

"I did?" Arnulf straightened up in his seat in surprise. "What gives you that impression?"

Winston's lip curled. "You were eager to tell us you have a case and weren't reluctant to share the nature of the matter when I asked."

My brother Harding once said: Men could often make things easier for themselves if they remembered their own words.

The farmer looked annoyed that he had played right into Winston's hand, but then his self-important look returned.

"Well, I don't suppose it can do any harm for you to hear about the case." He scooted forward in the seat, knees apart. "A month ago the wench was out on the heath looking after the sheep up there. Sometimes the lambs are born early, and I don't like to lose a lamb. The next day I rode up there along with three neighbors because we had some problems with wolves this winter. We successfully killed a couple on our way, finally reaching the sheep shelter. We were somewhat surprised to see a horse tethered to a Scotch broom shrub outside the shelter, so we rode closer with our spears at the ready."

Arnulf stopped to take a sip of his ale. I glanced around the hall. The women who had been cooking and the men who had been carving were all sitting now, eating slices of bread with meat on top. The slaves were sitting and eating with everyone else. The wench was half turned to us, and I noted the tension in her back muscles.

The farmer wiped the beer foam from his mustache and continued, "Well, we went closer and heard the wench's cries and squeals from inside the shelter. I was horrified when we got to her and saw the reason for all the noise, because a man was on top of her and had just finished bedding her. He jumped off as we came into view. When I scolded him for his misdeed, he just grinned, mounted his horse, and rode away."

I heard Alfilda stifle an exclamation, and I glanced at her in acknowledgment. The story didn't sound very plausible.

"You just let him ride away?" I said, shaking my head in disbelief.

His answer was terse. "What else could I do?"

Winston and I exchanged silent glances. Alfilda's face was so full of disdain that I was relieved it wasn't directed at me.

"Didn't she leave a mark on him?" I asked. Arnulf shook his head and said he didn't let his slaves bear arms.

"Not even a knife?" I wanted to know. But the answer was no.

"And now you're bringing a case against the rapist," Winston calmly interrupted before I could say anything more.

"He'll pay me the fine for the loss I suffered," Arnulf said, unable to hide a smug smile. "So far he has refused, but now it's up to the Hundred Court."

"Refused to pay?" Winston repeated, sounding tired.

"Refused to admit to committing the crime."

Now something dawned on me, so I asked, "Was the man a farmer?"

Arnulf snorted again and said, "Darwyn is his name, and he's the son of a thane."

Thanes, particularly young ones, tended to take a liberal view of farmers' rights, I knew all too well.

"And his father?" Winston asked.

"Delwyn, who owns a great deal of land not just in this hundred but all over East Anglia."

I opened my mouth, but Winston beat me to the question: "And what does this Delwyn say to the accusation against his son?"

"As thanes are wont to do, he believes his son over a farmer." Our host's lips twitched. "And yet this time he will be forced to bend."

I didn't understand. What made Arnulf so sure that the court would side with him?

"Your companions will swear in support of you?" Winston asked.

Now Arnulf laughed openly and replied, "Aye, that they will. It will be the word of four farmers against one thane."

Now I understood why he was so confident in his case. The thane wouldn't have had any trouble winning a case against one farmer, or even against three, but the word of four farmers carried more weight than the word of one thane. The law says that a man's word carries the same weight as his wergeld. That means 600 shillings for a landless thane, such as the young lawbreaker in question, and 200 for a farmer. So four farmers swearing together would tip the scales over this one Darwyn fellow.

"The fine for raping another man's slave is sixty-five shillings," our host smirked. "Plus the money the court will award me for the loss of her virginity."

It was dark out by the time our meal was over. We didn't linger at the table after the farmer's story, but thanked him right away, and were then shown to our sleeping places. Luckily we were not next to each other. I was sure I would hear Winston's snoring anyway, but at least it would be more muffled than if we were lying head to foot on the bench that ran along the side of the hall.

We hadn't exchanged a single word with the lady of the house, so we took pains to seek her out and thank her for the food, but she just nodded and went back to giving her girls orders.

I went outside in the cold spring evening to relieve my bladder. I couldn't stop thinking about the farmer who was so obviously looking forward to having his palm covered with silver the next day.

As soon as I'd realized the culprit was a thane, I had assumed the four spear-wielding farmers hadn't made the boy pay for his crime on the spot due to fear of the lad's kinsmen. Turns out I was wrong about that. They hadn't taken revenge on the spot because Arnulf was hoping to profit from the situation. He wasn't the first man I'd run into who was hungry for silver. As my brother Harding said: Men like that are as plentiful as sparrows flocking around horse droppings. And the rape hadn't even involved his wife or daughter, so it's not like he was required to seek revenge. He was free to merely appeal for reimbursement for his monetary loss.

Something else he'd said actually shook me more. When I was a boy, I was taught that noblemen are expected to take care of those in their employ, whether they be free farmers, serfs, or slaves.

A nobleman is only a nobleman, my father used to say, if he is magnanimous. I remember more than one occasion when my father drew his sword to defend one of his farmers' rights or to avenge a serf. I remember another time he hanged a neighbor's slave because the man had killed one of our own slaves. Of course, Father had offered to pay the wergeld for the slave, but our neighbor had not accepted since the hanged man had in fact killed our man.

Apparently Arnulf didn't share my father's view of things. True, Arnulf wasn't a nobleman, but a farmer, and yet such a man has the same obligations toward his subordinates as a nobleman has toward his.

And *he* was the one who sent a slave girl out into the heath, not just alone but also unarmed, even though he knew there were wolves.

5

The morning brought drizzly weather, thick porridge, and hot ale.

I had noted the drizzle through the door when I poked my head outside. Shivering, I decided my bladder could wait. The porridge slid down my gullet accompanied by the ale. And by the time I had my fill, the rain gave way to wisps of fog between the buildings.

I walked out to the paddock and saddled our horses. The red gelding greeted me with a nicker and nuzzled my hand, snorting and searching for the crust of bread I had sneaked into my pocket from one of the kitchen girls, who had been every bit as uncommunicative as her mistress.

I was tightening the girth beneath Alfilda's mare when Winston and she joined me, their arms full of odds and ends that they set about securing to the disagreeable Atheling's back.

"Are we leaving right away?" I made sure my hand couldn't slip under the girth. Two mornings earlier, Alfilda's woolly mare had tricked me by distending her belly as I attached the girth so that Alfilda's saddle had slipped downward as she rode.

Winston looked around, but we were alone in the paddock. Arnulf's people had saddled the farmer's horse for him while we were eating breakfast.

"We'll wait and ride together with the farmers," Winston said. They would be our cover when we rode into Thetford.

We led our nags out of the paddock and tied them to the post in front of Arnulf's hall. Two other horses already waited beside Arnulf's. We went back into the hall, and on seeing us from the hearth, Arnulf introduced us to the two men standing with him.

Herward was a portly, wispy-haired Saxon man with a long mustache and a potbelly held in place by a wide leather belt. He nodded when Arnulf introduced him, and his eyes lit up at the sight of Alfilda, although he quickly looked away at the fire.

His companion, Bjarne, was tall and strong, with extremely long auburn braids and a neatly trimmed, graying Danish beard. He also nodded at us and then immediately turned his eyes back to our host, who was listening to something outside the door, his head cocked.

We later learned that the Dane, Bjarne, owned an outlying farm a ways outside the village but still met his neighborly obligations to the little community.

The Saxon farmer, Herward, who was munching with great relish on a strip of cured meat, was master of one of the medium-sized farms we had noticed the day before. In addition to that, he confided to me between mouthfuls, he did quite a bit of trade in sheep.

Our host overheard this statement and informed us with a smile that he, too, knew a lot more about the sheep trade than about running a farm, which caused both Bjarne and Herward to laugh, though Herward's laughter sounded a little forced.

"When a man is as good a farmer as Arnulf, it's easy to poke fun at others who are not as fortunate," Bjarne said, brushing aside the kidding and holding his tankard out to a slave wench, who immediately refilled it.

After a while, we heard hoofbeats approaching. We all went out onto the green, which was bathed in cold morning light, to wait for the riders coming down from the hills.

A skinny Dane was in the lead, dressed in yellow breeches and a red linen shirt beneath an open doublet. He rode with the reins in his left hand and his spear in his right. His belt held a long knife, the polished-silver inlay of its bone handle gleaming in the sun.

Two others rode just behind him. On the left, a young lad who looked so much like the leader it had to be his son, and next to him, a heavyset Angle with a brown cape draped over his powerful shoulders.

The lady of the house must have been standing just inside the doorway of the hall because she instantly emerged with one of her girls in tow, presenting the new arrivals with steaming tankards. The refreshment was quite welcome, judging by how eagerly the contents disappeared down the three men's throats.

Although the morning was coming to an end, Arnulf invited us all back inside, as the rules of hospitality dictate, and we each received fresh tankards along with slices of bread topped with salted eel. It wasn't until we finished these that Arnulf introduced us to the new arrivals.

The Danish farmer's name was Sigvald, and he owned a farm about five miles to the west. His son, whose blond hair was cut short, was Sigurd. Their Angle companion owned a farm a bit south of theirs, and he was known as Alwyn of the Heath, he said, because the farm itself was up in the heathery knolls—although his land extended over the fertile ground bordering the marshland.

Sigvald did the talking, probably because he owned the largest farm. Sigvald's son didn't say anything, but his eyes were always on the move. The boy was vigilant, constantly scanning the hall to make sure all was well. Maybe despite his youth he knew that testifying against a thane's son wasn't the safest thing for a farmer to do.

Our host asked Alwyn if he had business before the court. Alwyn responded that since he was a man who mostly took care of things on his own, that was not the case. He said he was going to the market to collect on a debt. A sheep dealer had bought some of his animals at the Michaelmas market but had been allowed to postpone a portion of the payment, which was now due.

Winston explained what we were doing in the land of the East Anglians. Aside from the fact that Sigvald laughed condescendingly to learn that Winston made his living by filling pieces of parchment with lines and colors, the men accepted the story on face value: we were on our way to Saint Edmund's Town but wanted to spend a few days at the market in Thetford to see if Winston could add to his supply of inks and other items necessary for his work.

And so we rode toward Thetford as a large, well-armed group. The six farmers carried spears, which they held raised in their right hands with the shafts resting in a leather strap attached to their saddles. In addition, they all had decent knives in their belts, although none of the others' was as grand as Sigvald's.

They had all stolen glances at my sword, but none of them mentioned it or even asked where in the kingdom my lands were. Neither I nor my companions saw any reason to explain that the sword was the only thing that remained to show I'd been born the son of a thane.

Arnulf rode in the lead on his stocky gray mare alongside Sigvald, who was followed by Alwyn, who rode on his own. Behind him came the two farmers from the village, then Winston and Alfilda towing Atheling, who'd tried to demonstrate his dominance over one of the new horses, but had been emphatically put in his place by a bite on the neck. Now he was walking along obediently. Finally I brought up the rear along with Sigurd, who turned around in his saddle at regular intervals to look behind us.

"You're cautious," I noted. I, too, had been keeping a careful eye on our surroundings. It was prudent since we were riding with farmers who were planning to bring a case against a nobleman.

"Yes," he responded. Then the young farmer was quiet, keeping his eyes on the track ahead.

The day was now sunny and warm. I loosened my doublet and ran my hand down along my gelding's neck to make sure he wasn't sweating too much.

People occupied the road—a few with bundles on their backs, here and there a farmer's wife with chickens tied together at the legs dangling over her shoulders. A peddler or two hurried past to get to the market on time. Other travelers were on horseback, and all the riders moved along at a steady pace while the people on foot stepped aside, some of their own accord while others had to be asked to move out of the way. Our group maintained a good pace and reached the wooden palisade surrounding Thetford a bit before midday. Located at the confluence of the Thet and Little Ouse Rivers, the town had been burned to the ground only eight years earlier by King Sweyn after his victory at the Battle of Ringmere. It was mostly rebuilt now, however, apart from the town wall, which so far had been replaced with only the palisade.

We followed the Icknield Way to the easternmost of the town's three bridges, which were actually two bridges since the road, which crossed both rivers, formed its own bridge. This entrance was guarded by a fortification, which Winston said predated even the Romans. While we rode along under the watchful eyes of the guards, I realized the road had been routed this way because the crossing point was very easy to defend.

It was hard to tell that the town had been burned to the ground so recently. It seemed wealthy and bustling as we rode in and attempted to force our way through the throng of people. We rode through a meadow with a church at the far end and took a wide road to the center of town, passing yet another church and low buildings. It turned out Thetford was home to no fewer than five churches, with another two and a monastery just outside the palisade to the southeast—all evidence of the town's wealth. As we finally reached the church of Saint John, we found the marketplace before us.

We dismounted and pushed our way through the crowd, leading the horses by the reins. Our host had sworn he knew an inn that would have room for us since, as he put it, most of the people coming to sell things at the market preferred to sleep out in the open or in their stalls rather than spend money on shelter for the night.

Apparently he was right; at the inn across from Saint Mary's church, abutting the meadowlands along the river, the innkeeper obliged us. He was a skinny Angle by the name of Willibrord and, with an unending barrage of chatter, he escorted us to our beds. He almost made it seem like he'd been expecting us.

Winston and Alfilda were lucky and got one of the two third-floor rooms, where they had a window overlooking the meadow and a bed covered with thick blankets. I had to share my bed with

Sigurd in a room on the second floor, where Herward and Bjarne also had to squeeze into one bed. Sigvald, Alwyn, and Arnulf shared the other room on the third floor and were directly above us.

As soon as I'd put my things on the bed, I went downstairs and, following our host's directions, found the paddock that belonged to the inn. It bordered on the river on one side; a wattle fence lined the other three sides, with a gate to get in. The grass was green and inviting, and my red gelding bid me good-bye with a toss of his head followed by a loud neigh. Then he took a few playful leaps while Winston's and Alfilda's mares walked somewhat more calmly through the grass down to the river. They gave a couple of snorts and then began to drink.

When I returned, Winston had already unloaded everything from Atheling's back. I got out of having to tug the stupid beast down to the paddock because Sigurd had offered to do it. He was just gathering the reins for his father's and his own mounts in his right hand while holding Atheling's in his left.

I could tell from the mischievous glint in Atheling's eyes that he was looking to make trouble, but before I had a chance to warn Sigurd, the beast took the poor guy's shoulder in his teeth and gave him a hard shake, which I knew from firsthand experience was quite painful.

Sigurd howled in pain, twisted to the left, his shoulder still clenched. The young farmer kicked with all his strength straight upward between Atheling's forelegs, which made the mule bray temperamentally. But when the first kick was followed by a second, Atheling finally released Sigurd's shoulder, showed the whites of his eyes, and then allowed Sigurd to pull him away without any more fuss.

I smiled and called supportively to Sigurd that a good kick was just what that stupid mule needed. Then I entered the inn's tavern, where I found Winston and Alfilda seated at a long table.

I inquired about the whereabouts of our traveling companions. Winston said he didn't know where Alwyn was but that Arnulf and his group had gone across the river to where the Hundred Court was meeting in front of Saint Peter's church. They wanted to find out when their case would be heard.

Although the owner of the inn resembled a slender, thoroughly pruned alder trunk, it couldn't have been because of the inn's food, because the meal that was placed on the table before us was ample and the ale was good and nicely malted. The thick porridge from breakfast had long since disappeared from our stomachs, and we'd worked up a good appetite during the ride, so the three of us dug in.

The tavern's four long tables were crowded. Men and a few women helped themselves to ale, mead, and slices of bread topped with meat as they chatted or droned or yelled, depending on the speaker. Young girls scurried back and forth, serving the food and drink. At least two of them merited a lingering look from my eyes.

I had made short work of two tankards of ale and a thick slice of bread when Arnulf returned with his companions to announce that his case would be heard the next morning. We promised to attend as that was the only way we could thank him for his hospitality. Fond of money as he was, the rules of hospitality dictated that he must refuse payment for the lodging he'd offered us.

Since there wasn't room at the other tables, we offered to give them our spots and got up to head outside into the crowds. After all, we had a job to do.

6

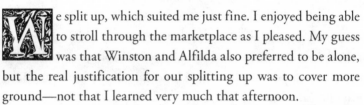e split up, which suited me just fine. I enjoyed being able to stroll through the marketplace as I pleased. My guess was that Winston and Alfilda also preferred to be alone, but the real justification for our splitting up was to cover more ground—not that I learned very much that afternoon.

Merchants and peddlers had set up stands, stalls, tents, and tables. Although they had plenty of rumors to share, very few of them had to do with kings or jarls. If I'd wanted information about the cloth, raw wool, hay, salt, horn spoons, honey, malt, or any of the other many goods that had been brought to Thetford by cart and wagon, horseback or handbarrow, I could certainly have learned as much as I wanted.

There was also knowledge to be had about the various reeves, thanes, and large farm holders—information essential to people doing business. Peddlers needed to know which thanes protected the roadways better and kept them free of highwaymen, as well as which large farm owners took their hospitality duties seriously, since that could mean the difference between lying in a bed with a blanket and sleeping out under the open skies. In contrast, people didn't believe kings or jarls had a direct impact on their lives. It was clear to both Winston and me, however, that they did;

kings and jarls truly laid the groundwork for all trade by guaranteeing the peace, or by failing to do so.

And peace did prevail in the land. You had to give that to Cnut. After the great national meeting in Oxford the year before, when the king had adopted the fundamental underpinnings of how the country would be governed, peace had prevailed between him and his noblemen, whether they had originated across the sea with him, or from among the local Danish population, or were descended from the Saxons, Angles, or Jutes who'd ruled this land since our distant ancestors had arrived with Hengist and Horsa.

Winston, Alfilda, and I knew, however, that the peace was a fragile one, as evidenced by the need for our secret mission. There wasn't a complete absence of conflict either, since noblemen were always getting into spats with each other, spats that were exacerbated during times of peace when their presence wasn't required on the battlefield, fighting either for or against the king.

As Harding used to say: Noblemen will bicker; it's part and parcel of who they are, and when ravens fight, the magpies are flayed.

This is why the king wanted strong jarls and reeves who could rein in disputes so that they didn't keep farmers from harvesting their crops or merchants from transporting their wares throughout the country. The king wanted trusted men who would keep a lid on the most contentious battles among noblemen so that only housecarls and salaried spearmen needed to be involved. Then the farmers wouldn't see their fields and farmhouses go up in smoke.

As I strolled through the market, I listened but didn't hear anything to suggest that Jarl Thorkell was once again engaged in any double dealings. Although, as I mentioned, that was probably because it wasn't the sort of rumor you would hear among merchants.

On the other hand, there was a lot to see at the market. Considering how early in the spring it was, the sun was nice and warm and shone brightly on all the exhibited wares. The rolls of cloth looked inviting and all the other high-quality goods were easier to admire in the sunshine than if there had been a dull spring rain soaking the stalls.

The lanes between the rows of displayed goods were narrow, and since the crowd acted the way every market crowd does, with people stopping at regular intervals to inspect a potential purchase more closely, it was slow going.

Not that I was in a hurry. I stopped now and then to look admiringly, not at cloth or the town's famed leather goods, but at girls who, with eager voices and inviting hand gestures, were better at selling than their husbands, fathers, and superiors.

One girl in particular drew my attention. A wench with a button nose, freckles, alluring hips, and inviting eyes gave me a sultry look even after I had turned down her offer to give me a discount on her goods.

I took up position across from her stall in the hope that she'd be called away on some errand so that I could offer to buy her a drink. But when she did finally step away, she ran straight into the arms of a rough-looking soldier who wrapped his arm around her possessively and led her away.

I hadn't given up on the drinking half of my idea, though, so I made my way to an ale stand. I had to step aside for a couple of soldiers who were hauling out a screaming dwarf. Then I sat down under the stand's awning at a long table that was wet with spilled ale.

I expressed my desire for a tankard of proper ale to a wrinkled old crone who listened and then snapped that that's all they sold since the town rules were strict on this point. She grumpily brought me a wooden tankard made of staves and a pitcher that smelled promisingly of malt.

The ale *was* good, I had to give it to her, and I enjoyed sitting at the table, watching people. A black-haired man with sharp-hewn features sat across from me. He was a few years older than I and wore a clean linen tunic beneath a well-maintained leather apron.

He glanced at me indifferently, but since I had the sense that he wasn't here for the market—which was for merchants rather than craftsmen—it occurred to me that he probably lived in town. He might be able to give me valuable information. So I politely drank to him and commented that business seemed brisk today.

He responded with a polite if somewhat reserved smile, but when I proceeded to praise the ale, good manners forced him to respond after all. And shortly thereafter I managed to draw him into the kind of casual conversation drinking men have with each other when they don't have any other company.

So it was natural enough that I offered him some of the ale from my pitcher after he had emptied the tankard he had ordered for himself. After a brief hesitation, he thanked me, and when I explained that I was a stranger in the town but was guessing he was from here, he nodded.

"I think I can guess your occupation," I told him with a smile.

"Really?" he responded aloofly.

"Yes. You're wearing a clean apron and your shirt is unstained. And"—I leaned forward and cocked my head toward a small hammer in his belt—"that suggests that you're a knife maker or possibly a silversmith. I'm wagering against a needle maker, because you seem too well dressed."

As soon as the words were out of my mouth, I realized that I'd put my foot in it. If he turned out to be a needle maker, he would hardly be pleased that I considered men of that profession shabby dressers. Luckily my guess had been right.

"You're almost right." The twinkle in his eye showed he'd loosened up.

"Aha, almost." I thought it over. What other professions did I know of that were related to the ones I'd mentioned? Comb maker? No, what would he need the hammer for? Armorer maybe, in charge of meticulous embellishments on swords? Metal chasing and repoussé?

He shook his head to each.

At any rate, I had him where I wanted him now because when I gave up, he would feel superior, and superior men are prone to letting their mouths run so as to maintain the upper hand.

"I am a journeyman with Erwin Mintmaster." He smiled briefly and raised his tankard. A powerful and important position, indeed.

"I'm Halfdan."

It remains unclear if he wanted to give me his name, because just then there was a commotion in the alley next to the ale stand. Six broad-shouldered spearmen pushed the crowd aside to make room for a dignified man with a gray beard whose power was evident from the guards who surrounded him and from the fact that he was on horseback within the marketplace whereas everyone else was on foot.

He was wearing a bright red cape over an embroidered tunic. His blue pants were tucked into stamped leather boots. His sword, worn in a belt inlaid with silver, had a gold hilt and an attractively embellished sheath. And his helmet, which he held in his right hand, gleamed with inlaid silver and was topped by a gold figure depicting a bear, which was clear even from a distance.

"A powerful man," I remarked.

My new acquaintance nodded.

"Maybe you know him?"

His response was another nod. Then he drained his tankard, stood up, and said, "My master awaits me."

Well, I hadn't learned anything from him, so I turned to a man behind me and tapped him on the back. When he turned his face to me, it was dark red with rage at my impertinence. I smiled as wide as I could and apologized for intruding. "But," I continued in my most polite voice, "I'm new here in town and hadn't realized I was disturbing a man of such importance, just as I'm not familiar with the nobleman who just rode by. I was hoping a man such as yourself might know him and be able to give me his name."

I don't know whether he responded because I'd flattered him or because he was happy to know something I didn't, but it didn't matter. The main thing was that I got the information I wanted.

The man decked out in silver was Turstan, thane and reeve, the man who would be deciding Arnulf's case tomorrow morning at the Hundred Court.

I returned to the tavern at the inn when the evening bell at Saint Mary's church rang. My companions were already enjoying a pot of stew, which smelled enticingly of rosemary.

One of the girls brought me an earthenware bowl. And since the flavor definitely lived up to the aroma, we sat in silence enjoying the lamb in cream sauce. I sopped up the last of the drippings with a slice of bread, and then pushed the bowl away.

"Not bad." I belched politely behind my hand and leaned across the table. "Not much of a rumor mill, that marketplace."

"No," Winston agreed, shaking his head. "We only picked up one item of interest."

I cocked my head.

"We had a drink at a stall where there was a Viking who'd had one too many."

I smiled. Now that was my kind of Viking. It's usually easy to get men like that talking.

"The king had revoked the man's shore leave—that's why he was here. He was on his way to join his shipmates back on board."

"So Cnut is calling his Vikings back to their ships because he's planning to start pillaging again?" I asked. Cnut had sent the majority of his Viking fleet home months ago, before the big meeting in Oxford, so he didn't currently have enough ships to engage in raids.

"No, the king isn't calling them back to pillage. According to our informant, Denmark is his goal."

Denmark? Cnut was going to leave his newly won kingdom and sail back across the sea to his homeland?

"Yes. There's news from Denmark. The king's brother Harold is said to be near death."

That explained it. If Harold Sweynsson died, Cnut was next in line for the kingdom of Denmark and it would be important for him to be in the country when the death occurred—or as soon as possible thereafter—so that he could be hailed king.

"So the king dreams of ruling a unified kingdom including England and Denmark, one that extends from the Baltic Sea to the Irish Sea?" I said.

"Harold doesn't have any sons," Alfilda explained. "So Denmark is free for the taking."

Now I saw what was going on more clearly. "Ah, so with the king at sea or back in Denmark, he'll need loyal men here in England."

Winston nodded and said, "In particular he needs to know that the most powerful of them all will keep his word."

Our errand in East Anglia suddenly took on an even greater importance.

7

I slept tolerably well. Sigurd moved around some in the bed, but an elbow in the side was all it took to get him to settle down. Herward was worse. His snoring would drown out even Winston's, but Bjarne quieted him with a few kicks. In the middle of the darkest hour, I heard Herward grunt, mutter something incoherent, and then roll over heavily to the sound of his bedmate's assurance that there could be "more where that came from."

In the morning, I took my morning piss by the paddock, where my red gelding greeted me with his friendly nicker. I was on my way to the wide washbasin behind the inn when two of my traveling companions rounded the corner of the building.

Arnulf had his hand on Sigurd's shoulder, and just as I ran into them, I heard him say that the matter would have to wait, since today was about getting his rightful money.

Sigurd blushed at the sight of me, stammered that he wouldn't be put off for much longer, and then turned on his heel while Arnulf confided to me that young people had no patience.

"Patience is a virtue, they say, but I believe it depends on the context," I replied casually. He didn't bite at my bait. Instead he nodded and then walked away.

After I scrubbed myself thoroughly and joined my companions at the long table, I became aware of my gnawing hunger and dug into the porridge with satisfaction. Unlike the previous day's, it was conspicuously supple from fat, and I washed it down with a good, malty ale.

Our travel companions joined us at the table, and Arnulf was in a lavish mood. He flirted with the wenches who served the porridge and ale, and laughed at almost every comment. He burped and wiped the porridge grease from the corners of his mouth, then smiled at Herward.

"A good day begins with a good meal," he crowed and continued, "and it will look lighter for us this evening than yesterday."

Herward nodded while Bjarne dryly stated that the evenings always got lighter in the spring, and the rest of us agreed.

Guards stood at the bridge over the river from the southern part of town. The soldiers questioned everyone closely, so only those who had legal matters for the court gained access. While we waited, a town resident who claimed to live behind Saint Peter's church was turned away, told he would have to come back after the court was adjourned.

Although Alwyn didn't have any business before the court, he came with the rest of us to be neighborly, as he put it. So Arnulf stepped before the court with a considerable entourage.

Soldiers armed with spears lined the square in front of the church. A platform had been erected in front of the church's wide front door, and the reeve I'd seen the day before sat there, enthroned on a broad chair. To the right of the platform, six spears stuck into the ground outlined a small square area. To the left, two spears at each end demarcated a rectangle.

The men who had come from throughout the hundred to observe the proceedings stood in a semicircle within the square. The arc of men began halfway down the church wall behind the reeve and ran all the way around to end in the corresponding spot on the other side.

When we arrived, the Hundred Court was hearing a case against a burly farmer, who stood calmly inside the area fenced in by the spears regarding his accusers—two other farmers, who alleged that he had changed the boundary line between their properties.

When the accusers were quiet, Reeve Turstan looked toward the farmer, who claimed he could bring in good men as witnesses that the boundary stone hadn't been budged, but to the contrary had sat in the same place for as long as anyone could remember.

The reeve looked out over the assembly and asked in a voice accustomed to being heard over the din of battle whether anyone wanted to swear in support of either the accusers' or the defendant's account. Three farmers stepped forward.

Once they had sworn in support of the defendant's words, the reeve asked if anyone wanted to swear for the accusers. This time one lone old man stepped forward and claimed under oath that, based on what his grandfather had told him, the boundary stone had been further in on the accused's property back during the reign of Æthelstan Half-King. This claim was met by cries from some of the assemblymen that this old man was known for his inability to remember things or think clearly.

The reeve then asked if there was anyone else present who could swear in this case, but when no one stepped forward, the court's verdict was that the accusers had not supported their case, so the boundary stone was where it should be.

We watched as the reeve heard several other cases, and then it was Arnulf's turn to step within the six spears. In a firm voice he called out that he had a case against Darwyn, son of Delwyn, involving the rape of a previously untouched slave maid.

Turstan looked out over the assembly and asked Darwyn to step forward. There was a commotion as a few men pushed their way through.

A nobleman's lad of scarcely twenty with blond, well-groomed hair, and broad cheekbones and shoulders stepped into the spot for the accused. He wore expensive, well-made clothes. His sword, whose hilt was unadorned, hung from a silver-draped belt, which also contained a horn-handled knife.

An older version of the lad took up position behind him. This man was wider around the waist and shoulders, with a neck that would have been at home on a bull. The older man had a long, gray-tinged mustache, and a look that said he would not yield to anyone.

The reeve acknowledged his and his son's presence with a polite nod and bade Arnulf to present his case, which he did in an exemplary fashion and—to my surprise—without allowing his hunger for silver to shine through at any point.

Arnulf succinctly recounted the story we had previously heard in his hall. Then he explained that he was demanding not just a fine for the crime, but also reimbursement for the loss of the girl's virginity. At this, Delwyn's left hand dropped down to the leather pouch that hung from his sword belt.

Arnulf's words were met with silence from the assemblymen. Not the brooding, ominous silence that someone who unjustly accuses another would encounter, but the silence of men who are familiar with the case and find it as uninteresting as it is obvious.

Turstan turned directly to Darwyn and asked in a bored voice, "And does the accused acknowledge his guilt?"

Arnulf's grin—no doubt a result of envisioning the silver he would soon be awarded—disappeared quickly when Darwyn loudly stated that he was not guilty of the accusation.

I looked from Arnulf to Darwyn, but it was his father's expression that struck me. Disbelief and uncertainty fought for control of his face. Then Delwyn took half a step back and stood, his face stony, while the reeve's voice cut through the agitated murmur among the assemblymen: "And you have people willing to testify under oath to this?"

"Under oath, yes," Darwyn said, sneering at Arnulf. For his part, Arnulf's red face revealed his confusion. Darwyn called someone named Bardolf, and a nobleman's son stepped forward.

He hardly looked old enough to use a weapon, but a sword hung at his hip, and his voice was firm as he swore his oath and attested that he knew Darwyn was not guilty of the charge directed against him.

Bardolf's words had scarcely died away before a commotion rose behind the accused. Delwyn, who had been standing behind his son, turned on his heel and left the court area accompanied by three men.

Turstan's lips curled. "And you, Arnulf," he said. "You have men who will swear for you?"

Herward, Bjarne, and Sigvald stepped forward and swore their oaths that on the day in question, which they stated, at the specific location, which they described, Darwyn had raped the slave girl, Guthild.

"And that is your testimony?" The reeve's lips curled again. Arnulf nodded.

Turstan rose from his chair and looked out over the assembly. "Are there any others who can swear under oath in this case?"

He waited a moment, but when no one stepped forward, he declared that thanks to Bardolf's sworn corroboration, Darwyn had refuted the accusation and therefore the case was dead and considered dropped.

Winston, Alfilda, and I expected Arnulf to be furious at the judge, to scream about injustice, and to lament the loss of the compensation he had been so sure he would receive. But none of that happened.

He allowed himself to be led away from the court in disbelief by Bjarne and Sigvald. He followed them through the rows of assemblymen, who parted to let him through. He remained silent until we reached the tavern. Then he shook off Bjarne's and Sigvald's hands and declared, his voice cracking, that this judgment nullified all agreements.

"This injustice undoes everything; no pact or agreement can persist when the law permits this." Arnulf grasped at the air, as if the law were a thing he could capture. He looked at his companions, who watched him in silence. Sigurd was pale with agitation; he was still young enough to feel the injustice viscerally. Herward bit his lip, Bjarne sighed thoughtfully, and Sigvald shook his head with sorrow. Only Alwyn seemed unaffected and mumbled that you had to be prepared for things like this if you wanted to go face-to-face with big fish. That, he said, was why he had never brought a case against anyone.

Arnulf said that he was going to ride home, but then the others said they might as well see what the market had to offer since they were here. After a brief discussion Arnulf let himself be convinced to remain in Thetford until the next day. He reluctantly joined his companions in a visit to the market.

The rest of us headed into the tavern, where we found a quiet corner to drink our tankards of ale. Alfilda drank thirstily and then set her tankard down with a little clunk. "Farmers always seem to lose when they go up against noblemen," she remarked.

I opened my mouth to respond, but Winston beat me to it. "In this case only when noblemen are willing to perjure themselves. I've been to many assembly meetings, but this is the first time I've ever seen someone swear falsely."

Alfilda vigorously shook her head. "I didn't mean it like that. Noblemen use the power they have."

"True." I met her eyes in agreement. "But swearing a false oath before the court is rare. It makes a man a nithing, a weak, unmanly coward. So, it basically never happens."

"And yet we just saw it happen," Alfilda retorted. She was angry, her cheeks pale.

Winston placed his hand on hers, but she brushed him away.

"Alfilda," Winston said, biting his lip. "Those two have made their bed. Eventually they're going to have to lie in it."

I saw her look of skepticism and explained, "No one has any doubt that Darwyn and Bardolf perjured themselves. You heard Turstan's voice. You watched Delwyn walk away when his son brought shame to him and his kin. Delwyn was as convinced of Darwyn's guilt as everyone else. I saw Delwyn reach for his money pouch. I almost had the impression he was willing to pay before the case even got started."

"So why did they do it?" Alfilda asked.

"Darwyn and Bardolf are too young to realize what they've done." Winston tugged on his nose. "A man must swear to something if he is sure. Take the old man in the case of the boundary stone. True, he may be feeble and forgetful, but he was convinced that his memory was correct. And I'm sure you remember the case in Oxford when a murderer stood there on his own before the king's meeting because everyone knew he was guilty, so no one would swear with him.

"That's justice: honest men's oaths are true and binding, because dishonest men will be found out and shunned by their neighbors and associates. There is no worse word that a man can be labeled with than the one Halfdan just used: nithing.

"But those two young pups don't get it. They think their noble lineage gives them rights because it gives them power. That boy had the power to rape that girl. Lord knows, many noblemen have abused their power, and more will follow. But at the Hundred Court, free men speak the truth because truth is the basis of law.

"Believe me, I wish I were a mouse beneath Delwyn's floor today so that I could hear what he has to say to his son. I'd hazard to guess that by nightfall Darwyn will have realized that he lost the respect not only of all decent men but also of his own father today."

Winston took a drink.

After a pause, Alfilda quietly asked, "So, Arnulf lost his right to the money. But what about the girl? What is her right? Or does a slave not have any rights?"

"I believe our young nobleman here can better answer that than I," Winston said with a glance at me.

I cleared my throat and began, "The girl's rights were trounced by a money-hungry master. Yes, slaves have rights. The law protects them by stipulating a fine for their rape or murder, for example. If Arnulf hadn't been so greedy for silver, he would have killed Darwyn when he found him committing the rape. With three witnesses, he would have been well within his rights when he came upon that whelp with his pants down and his cock in the girl. So one could say that Arnulf's rights were trounced by the lie Darwyn told today, and the slave girl's rights were trounced by a master who chose to seek monetary damages instead of revenge."

Alfilda studied my face with her gray eyes. Then she stated, "You would have killed him."

It wasn't a question. All the same, I replied: "Yes, I would have killed him."

8

umor of Darwyn's and Bardolf's perjury had spread through the marketplace like a fire.

I'd left Winston and Alfilda and gone off to be alone. And everywhere I went the topic of conversation was the morning's court business. I didn't hear a single voice raised in defense of the two young noblemen.

To the contrary, everyone denounced them; even a poor peddler, whose entire inventory consisted of three bundles that could fit in his pockets, spat on the ground at the mention of them. A benevolent-looking young man dressed like a priest lectured some women that the Lord himself had told people not to bear false witness against a neighbor, so old English law was just as divine as the one Moses had brought down from the mountain.

I strolled down one marketplace walkway after another, then turned onto a random street, followed it to the end, and wandered back into another narrow passage, glancing at the girls and the wares on display without seeing either a wench or a market stall that enticed me.

As the bells chimed midday, I recognized the man I'd met in the same ale stand the day before and took a seat across from him. When the crone who worked there came scurrying over, I asked for a pitcher of ale and noted that she had not grown any friendlier.

"So, Erwin Mintmaster must be a generous master," I said over the table as my ale was placed in front of me.

My black-haired acquaintance, who hadn't looked up until now, seemed confused, wondering if he knew me and who I was. He furrowed his brow for a second, and then recognition came into his eyes as he apparently remembered our short meeting the day before. But he raised his eyebrows questioningly, as if wondering what I'd meant by my comment.

"Well, he gives you so many opportunities to enjoy your ale," I explained in a lighthearted tone.

He responded, "Erwin is a witness at the court." His voice did not sound easygoing and approachable, as mine had.

I understood. Striking the king's coins involves stringent standards: No coin may be struck unless the mintmaster himself is present, since he is personally responsible for ensuring that all coins are pure and unadulterated. Work has to be paused any time an errand calls him away from the workshop.

"Nothing serious, I hope." I brushed aside his dismissive attitude.

"The mintmaster is not bringing the case. He is the king's trusted man and therefore has to attend all matters presented at the court." You could hear the journeyman's pride in his master's importance.

I made my voice sound impressed: "And you are his senior journeyman?"

"His journeyman."

Although Thetford was a significant town, its mint was not as large as London's or Winchester's.

"A trusted position."

His response was a nod.

"My name is Halfdan."

"You said that yesterday."

Ah, so he had been listening.

"And I work for Winston the Illuminator."

Now he looked at me in astonishment. "Work for?"

I stifled a smile. Clearly, he'd thought I was a thane and had been reluctant to open up too much to me because he was uncertain why a nobleman would show so much interest in him.

"I'm his man, yes, while I wait to come into my own."

But he didn't care about me or my lost entitlements. Winston's name was obviously familiar to him.

"Winston the Illuminator, who illustrated the Ely monastery's book about Saint Etheldreda?"

That certainly sounded like something Winston might have done and since my new acquaintance seemed impressed, I said, "The same."

"A very handsome book. I saw it last winter when my master and I had business in Ely." He sat up straighter and smoothed his apron. "My name's Harold."

Then he seemed to loosen up and gladly accepted a tankard from my pitcher. His more relaxed manner was not due to my winning nature, however. Instead it seemed to stem from knowing that he was with someone close to Winston.

Naturally his first question had to do with what had brought us to Thetford. He bought my story about the work awaiting my master in Saint Edmund's Town as well as my explanation that we were stopping in Thetford so that Winston could stock up on paints and other materials. After that he started asking about Winston's work and seemed sincerely puzzled that I couldn't answer his questions, but he lit up when I promised that I would introduce him to Winston so that he could ask him in person. And he was willing to answer all of my questions.

His master obviously confided in him, because he knew all sorts of things a general journeyman tradesman normally wouldn't.

A mintmaster is a trusted man. The opportunity to weigh out the correct amount of silver and stamp the king's image on it as a guarantee of the coin's value is not given to just anyone, particularly men who are not even of noble blood.

A mintmaster answers to the king, but since the king's wishes are enforced by his jarls, a mintmaster—and thereby his journeyman—gains firsthand knowledge of how the biggest squires in the land are getting along.

My good Harold was also able to confirm Winston's sense that Cnut would not wait long before heading to Denmark to assert his claim to the land should his brother die. In fact, he informed me that his master had been summoned to see the king. Cnut made the mintmaster swear an oath that he would not strike coins in any name other than Cnut's for the next three years.

Harold, as a common tradesman, did not realize the significance of this information. I, on the other hand, immediately saw that the king, by requiring this oath, had put up obstacles, should Thorkell consider overthrowing him during his absence.

If a jarl wanted to seize power, he would of course need to be able to guarantee the tradespeople their profits. Such a guarantee would require issuing coins that bore the jarl's name, thereby showing that he controlled the land's monetary system.

Such power could be used or abused. A jarl who wished to undermine his king could allow impure coins to be made and inundate the market with such poor quality money that he destroyed the confidence merchants, tradespeople, farmers, and noblemen had in the currency. Once the distrust was sowed, the collapse of the country's economy would not be far off, and that would throw the entire country into disarray. The whole place would then be up for sale to the strongest bidder—almost always the contender who was physically present in the country.

The jarls and the king all knew this, and now Cnut had secured the mintmaster's word that Thorkell couldn't just lie to Erwin Mintmaster, telling him the king was dead. Cnut was wise to realize that people can't be prevented from lying. Even mintmasters would believe a sufficiently substantiated claim that the king had died abroad in his homeland. That's why Cnut had required a three-year oath.

If Jarl Thorkell should get it into his head to engage in treachery—yet again—the king would be back from Denmark before Thorkell had a chance to print his own coins in his own name.

I agreed with Harold's explanation, asked a couple of trivial questions, and was just about to see if the journeyman knew where Thorkell was when a man sat down heavily on the bench beside me.

It was Arnulf, and he had very clearly been drowning his legal defeat in malty ale. His bloodshot eyes were narrowed, his clothes disheveled, and when he opened his mouth to announce his presence, his voice was slurred.

I saw the men who had sworn in support of his testimony behind him. Sigvald, Herward, and Bjarne all appeared to be sober, although Arnulf's drunken state did not seem to bother them.

"Could we leave him with you?" Sigvald asked. "The rest of us would like to do some shopping, but that has not been possible so far."

I owed Arnulf this much after the hospitality he'd shown us, so I nodded with an apologetic glance at Harold, who shrugged and got up, commenting that he had to get back to the workshop anyway to see if the apprentice had cleaned up as he'd been ordered to do.

Arnulf ordered himself a pitcher of ale and tossed a coin onto the table. He rested a heavy hand on my shoulder, and mumbled that the world would see he wouldn't just put up with whatever. Then he belched loudly and tried unsuccessfully to lift the pitcher. He was forced to set it back down, sloshing. Then he slumped over and fell asleep with his head resting on the table.

The old crone came over immediately, but I waved her away, promising that I would remove him as soon as I'd emptied the pitcher he'd paid for. Then I spent a good while drinking his ale and making sure his head didn't roll off the edge of the table.

When the afternoon was half over, I hoisted him up and with great difficulty managed to lead him through the narrow streets. We had to stop once so that he could piss behind a tree, but I refused to help him arrange his clothes again afterward, so I reached the inn with a somewhat sorry-looking farmer.

A group of spearmen stood guard outside the inn, and I stopped short when I recognized their leader, who pulled his sword at the sight of me and my burden.

"Arnulf," Delwyn said gruffly. "So you took your revenge."

9

A gurgling sound warned me just as Arnulf retched, and I managed to jump aside from the vomit, which splashed onto the ground right where I had stood. Delwyn took a step forward, his cheekbones white and his lips pursed. The tip of his sword pointed right at the farmer, and his eyes were as wan as the steel of the blade.

Arnulf burped hollowly, emitted another jet of vomit, and swayed, moaning faintly before he straightened himself up. With watering eyes he stared in terror at the thane.

I saw Delwyn's look of determination and his sword, which he had raised up in preparation. In a moment he would swing the blade at the farmer's neck. Arnulf moaned in fear, grabbed my arm, and pulled me toward him. Then we both teetered together in a grotesque dance, our eyes on Delwyn's sword, me trying to get free, Arnulf in horrified anticipation of the blow that would strike him as soon as I managed to do so.

I finally tore myself loose with a jerk, and Arnulf collapsed, whimpering. Delwyn stepped forward again, brought the sword back behind his shoulder, and tensed his muscles to swing it when a voice stopped him.

"Are you the judge and the executioner, thane?" asked Winston.

I looked over the spearmen's shoulders and saw Winston and Alfilda standing on the inn's stairs. Delwyn hadn't moved a muscle but replied without taking his eyes off the whimpering Arnulf that a man was judged by his deeds and that a nobleman took his own revenge without inconveniencing an executioner.

"True enough," agreed Winston. He calmly descended the steps, broke through the line of spearmen, and positioned himself between Delwyn and Arnulf. "And you have reason to take revenge against Arnulf?"

Only now did Delwyn look up, his gaze falling on Winston.

"Step aside," Delwyn ordered.

"If you have reason to take revenge, of course I will step aside," said Winston, not even deigning to glance at me. "But perhaps an explanation would be in order."

Delwyn snarled, then lowered his sword. He was obviously no less angry, but his muscles were quivering from strain and needed a rest.

"My son was murdered."

Of course we had both guessed that much.

"I'm sorry to hear that," Winston said, bowing his head respectfully. "How?"

Delwyn took a deep breath, which hissed out from his pressed-together lips.

"He was found stabbed"—Delwyn paused, inhaling in puffs, before he continued in a growl—"under a piece of canvas at the market."

"And witnesses saw Arnulf kill him?" Winston asked calmly.

"You're not hearing what I'm saying. His body was found under a piece of canvas."

"So there are no witnesses," Winston surmised.

"I don't need witnesses. Only one man has reason to kill my son."

Winston nodded, then turned to address me. "You were with Arnulf."

I saw what he was getting at. Still, I wasn't sure I wanted to swear to Arnulf's innocence, so I turned to Delwyn and asked, "When was your son found?"

"Shortly after the midday bell, a shopkeeper walked into his storeroom at the market and found his body." Delwyn stared angrily at me.

I glanced at Winston, who responded by raising his eyebrow at me and grunting. "Well?"

"I was not with Arnulf then." I briefly recounted how Arnulf's companions had deposited him with me. "So I have been with him for the time it takes to empty a pitcher of ale."

Arnulf's whimpering had subsided. Now he was trying to stand up, but one look from Delwyn made him sink back down again.

"Before that he was with his companions?" Winston asked.

"Presumably," I said with a shrug.

"A presumption we ought to investigate," Winston said and turned to Delwyn. "If there are witnesses to Arnulf's innocence, you will have to seek your revenge elsewhere."

Delwyn's response was a disdainful snort.

"No one else had any unfinished business with my son," he snarled.

"Not that you know of." Winston thought for a moment. "Shortly after the midday bell, you said. Evening is approaching now. You've taken your time."

The thane flung out his left hand in anger and grumbled, "It took a while for them to identify my son and then I had to be found."

"You were at the market, you said?" Winston asked me, tugging on his nose.

I knew what he wanted to find out.

"I didn't hear about a murder, but it's a big marketplace and I was engrossed in conversation at an ale stand."

"Where is this storeroom?" Winston asked Delwyn, who turned to look at one of his spearmen.

"Uh, it's more like a tent," the muscular soldier rumbled. "It's all the way out by the edge of the market down by the meadow."

We were interrupted by the sound of running and turned around. The three farmers who had left their drunken companion with me came scurrying toward the inn, spotted us, and stopped abruptly.

"So you've heard the news," Sigvald said. When he saw Delwyn, he uttered a faint "uh." He looked at Arnulf, still huddled on the ground. "Why . . . ?"

No one responded, but after a moment I saw a flicker of understanding dawn in his face.

"Yes, but . . ." Sigvald began. He stared from Winston to Delwyn in confusion and then at me. "You don't believe that he . . . ? He couldn't have . . ."

Winston gave Sigvald a look of encouragement.

"Arnulf was with us, of course," Sigvald explained.

"And you're willing to swear to that?" Winston's eyes were on Delwyn now, who was contemplating Sigvald with a look of puzzlement on his face.

Sigvald looked at his companions, who both nodded. "We'll swear to that. Arnulf was with us from the time we left the inn here until we left him with Halfdan."

"I demand that you swear to that," Delwyn said, biting his lip.

Again the farmers nodded and without hesitation all three raised their right hands and swore that Arnulf could not have committed the crime, because he was with them the entire day until they met me at the ale stand.

Thane Delwyn listened to their oaths in silence, then resheathed his sword without a word, and gestured with his head to his spearmen, who obeyed and followed his heavy steps away.

We watched them disappear down a street, and then Winston turned to the still-kneeling Arnulf.

"You can get up now."

Arnulf got to his knees, sniffling, wiped the snot and spit from his lips, and then stood and walked up the stairs with his head bent, side by side with his companions. He left a wet spot in the dust where he'd been sitting.

Winston looked at me and said, "So you would step aside to allow a farmer to be cut down."

I saw no reason to respond to that.

10

Later that evening we gathered at the long table in the tavern. "We" being the group that had ridden to Thetford together, aside from Arnulf, who remained up in the room he was sharing with Sigvald and Alwyn of the Heath. According to Alwyn, Arnulf was snoring in his bed.

"And you're sure he wasn't drinking to forget that he'd killed a man?" I couldn't shake the thought that Arnulf was the only person I knew who had any reason to want Darwyn dead.

"He was drinking to forget the court had ruled against him," Sigvald said harshly.

There was a glint in Alfilda's eye as she leaned forward and asked, "Was it the ruling he took so hard or not receiving the silver?"

"They're one and the same to Arnulf," Sigvald said with a wry look in his eyes, but then his expression hardened. "You could just as well ask whether Darwyn perjured himself to save his reputation or to save his father from paying the fine."

Alfilda was going to respond, but Winston's hand on her arm held her back.

"Let it go," he said.

"But . . ." Alfilda began, but then she sighed and tucked into the food that had been placed in front of us.

We hadn't finished dinner yet when heavy footsteps on the stairs made us look up.

Arnulf didn't look much better than when he'd gotten up off the dusty ground outside. His hair was matted, and his shirt drooped out over his belt. He had, however, changed into a clean, dry pair of pants, his mouth was free of vomit, and although his eyes were bloodshot, he had the haughty look of a man hiding his shame by pretending not to care what anyone else thought.

All eyes were on him as he walked across the room, the floor creaking beneath his weight. When he reached us, Sigvald and Herward made space between them, but Arnulf shook his head.

"I'm going out for a minute."

Winston and I exchanged glances. True, it wasn't any of my business if Arnulf tempted fate by leaving the safety of the inn. Delwyn might believe Arnulf's companions were telling the truth and that he was innocent of the murder, but the thane didn't have anyone else to exact his revenge on, and if their paths crossed tonight, I wasn't sure Arnulf would feel so safe then.

Sigvald must have agreed with me, because he sounded concerned when he asked if that was wise.

"Wise?" growled Arnulf. "Good men swore that I couldn't have committed the crime. Surely even for a thane, one perjury a day is enough."

At this point I thought it was about time to get to the truth, and although Winston warned me against it with a shake of his head, I pointed out that Delwyn had not been guilty of any improper conduct.

Arnulf shot me a scornful look and said, "So you're saying that a man who stands by and allows his son to perjure himself is behaving as a thane should?"

I realized it was pointless to respond, so I simply shrugged before turning my attention back to the food.

But Arnulf didn't feel like letting it go.

"You carry a sword and act like a nobleman," he said, "so who cares what you think about this case?"

A flush of rage spread up my neck, and I put my hands on the edge of the table to stand up and give him a piece of my mind, but Winston beat me to it.

"Just go, Arnulf, if that's what you want to do," Winston said.

Arnulf hesitated a couple of seconds, his breathing labored. Then he slowly walked toward the door and disappeared out into the spring night.

As I sat with my hands hovering above the table, my body was tense with anger. Everyone at the table remained silent until Sigvald sighed.

"You have to excuse him, Halfdan," he said.

"I do?" I cleared my throat to get the tension out of my voice. "For what? For thinking that all thanes are like the one who perjured himself, or for accusing me of letting a man's lineage determine whether he's trustworthy?"

"The law already made that decision," Sigvald said bitterly.

I was silent and tried to quell my rage. Then I took a deep breath and nodded.

Sigvald pushed the bench back. The farmers were leaving the table. Sigvald and his son walked toward the door. Alwyn glanced up the stairs, and then he followed Herward, who also disappeared out the door after a brief exchange of words with Bjarne. Bjarne stood for a bit, but after an indifferent glance at us, he walked past us to a table with three men who willingly made room for him and drew him into their conversation.

I noticed Winston looking at me. He seemed cheerful.

"You should stop acting like a thane if you want to hang out with farmers," he teased.

I glared at him.

"Just let it go." Winston flung up his hands, which he then let settle down into Alfilda's lap. "Let's head upstairs," he suggested to her.

That suited me just fine. I needed to be alone, but before I had a chance to get up, a shadow fell over the table.

"Halfdan! I thought I'd probably find you here," Harold said.

I looked up at him. A stout man wearing a blue tunic under a beautifully stitched leather vest and bright crimson wool breeches stood behind him. He eyed Winston. The man looked calm and approachable and yet a bit guarded.

"This is my master, Erwin Mintmaster," Harold said. He had taken off his apron as a sign that the workday was over.

I bowed slightly to them and then realized what had brought them to the tavern.

"And this is my master, Winston the Illuminator, and his lady friend, Alfilda."

Erwin bowed and asked me in a surprisingly cheerful voice if they could join us. Winston nodded his consent and when a girl came bustling over, the mintmaster ordered four tankards of ale and then looked questioningly at Alfilda, who with a quick smile requested a goblet of mead.

I didn't really want to stick around and listen to the two coin makers heaping praise on my master for his work. So I put a hand on the girl's arm and said, "Three tankards will do."

I got up, nodded to the others and said, "You'll have to excuse me."

Harold looked at me in astonishment, while Winston shook his head sharply and confided in the others that I usually liked to go skirt chasing once my stomach was full.

My first instinct was to make some biting retort, but then I realized that his accusation spared me from having to come up with an excuse. So I nodded yet again and walked toward the door, letting it swing closed behind me.

The evening was a little chilly, now that the sun was no longer strong and there was a dark-blue, cloudless sky above us. The moon was full, so the town was lit by golden moonlight, which made the shadows stand out.

The selling was done for the day, but that didn't mean that the marketplace was quiet. Laughter, shouting, and raised voices came from the ale stands. The reeve's guards made their rounds through the market aisles, and squeals and amorous voices came from a few tents where whores were helping extract silver from lustful men's pockets.

I stood for a bit, allowing my rage to cool. Then I walked down to the paddock where my red gelding greeted me and snorted into my shirt in the hope of finding some oats or a crust of rye bread.

The moon was just overhead and my shadow was short as it fell on the grass. I patted the gelding's neck. It was dumb to get worked up about the farmer's words, but his affront had been clear: I carried a sword, but even though I rode a well-fed horse and wore more expensive clothes than a farmer, I was not a thane, which stung.

Then suddenly a thought struck me: What would my word be worth at court? I was no farmer, and a thane by lineage only, as the king had refused to give me land. I was a free man, but I had chosen to serve a master and was paid by him and by the king.

Cnut's reasons for denying me land were blatantly obvious: He knew that once I owned land and a farm, I would live as a thane and no longer serve Winston. If I wasn't serving Winston, I would no longer serve the king, who would therefore be short a bloodhound. A detective, after all, was worth more to him than one thane among countless others.

The red gelding snorted against my neck, and I did what he wanted, patting him again. To hell with the traitorous Eadric the Grasper, who had abandoned his own leader midbattle and sealed the victory for Cnut by switching to his side. It had cost my father and my brother their lives, and me my inheritance and birthright.

I shuddered, shaking off thoughts that would lead to nothing. Destiny requires you to follow the path you're on.

But the path could be altered, if you set your mind to it. For me that meant holding out until the day when King Cnut owed me so much that he would have to award me an estate, land, and honor again.

I gave the gelding one last pat, and then slowly walked toward the market, contemplating whether I felt like stopping at an ale stand and spending the rest of the evening in the company of some drinking mates who wouldn't mean a thing to me tomorrow, or if I should bite the bitter apple and return to those I'd left at the tavern and spend the evening listening to the coin makers fawn over Winston. I had just decided that neither option was particularly appealing when I heard footsteps come running, wheezing and panting, and someone swearing.

I grabbed for my sword, but before my hand reached the hilt, I was knocked over as someone darted around the corner and slammed into my chest. I cursed, slipped on a cow patty, and struck the dirt with a grunt, which became even louder as the person who'd smashed into me landed on my stomach.

I cursed and flung my arms around the person, tossed them aside, and scrambled to my feet just as two dark silhouettes came thundering around the corner. My sword was drawn and my legs firmly planted, ready to meet them. Meantime I hoped the person I'd tossed aside wouldn't pounce on me from behind, and I barked that the new arrivals should freeze. Immediately!

The moonlight illuminated a couple of scruffy-looking soldiers. The one on the left wore threadbare breeches and a vest that had seen better days. His face was bright red, surely as much from drink as from the exertion of running. The one on the right didn't look much better. He was missing his left eye, wore ragged clothes, and breathed in gasps so that his bad breath lingered around him in a cloud.

Neither of them carried a sword, I determined with relief.

"What seems to be the problem?" I decided to deal with these two first but kicked around to locate the fallen person just to be safe. I moaned reflexively as the tip of my toe struck the fallen figure's ribs.

The two shabby soldiers stared at each other indecisively. It was a good sign that even from the beginning they lacked confidence. As Harding said: A man should always act confident. You need to believe you will be victorious in order to win.

"Well?" I prompted, staring hard to increase their uncertainty.

"Uh, sir." The man's bad breath hit me. "She, uh . . ."

"Yes?"

"Uh, we . . ."

So apparently I had prevented a rape, which seemed just, considering what had taken place at the court earlier in the day.

"You just decided to find a different companion," I completed the man's sentence for him.

He stared uncertainly at his buddy, who sized me up. So I whipped the tip of my sword up a little, which was enough. They left with their tails between their legs.

I waited until their footsteps had completely died away, then walked around the corner to peer down the narrow lane. Only after determining that no one else was around did I turn back toward the men's intended victim.

She did not seem to appreciate my help, sitting there in the dust, arms clutched to her chest. To my delight, I saw that she was only a bit younger than I am, maybe eighteen summers old. She was wearing a gray dress, and had a clean, friendly face, which was now blushing.

"You kicked me," she sulked. She had a pleasant voice.

"And hit you in the chest, I see," I said, grinning at her.

I held my hand down to her. She glared at it angrily, but then she took it and allowed me to pull her up. She came up to my chin, her blonde braids hanging down to her waist, and in her eyes there was an invitation that had been hidden by anger.

"Did I break your breastbone?" I asked.

She grimaced in pain, but shook her head.

"It hurts, though."

"More than if those two scoundrels had gotten ahold of you?" I asked, almost with a chuckle.

She shook her head. "They were lying in wait for me when I came out of the market stall."

"You own a stall?" She didn't look like she owned much.

Turns out I was right. "Can a woman own anything?" she spit out scornfully, then her voice changed, becoming charming as she explained, "I was just tidying and closing up, because my husband went to the ale tent."

"Husband?"

She nodded and added, "My husband is very fond of the ale tent."

I cursed my luck that when I had finally played the part of noble rescuer, it was to a married woman. Then the import of her words and tone sank in.

"So he'll be in there for a while?" I asked.

"And then he'll return to our stall, where he prefers to sleep." Now her invitation was clear.

"Maybe we should check you over and make sure you don't have a broken rib." I reached out to lay the back of my hand against her cheek.

"I think that would be best." She grabbed my hand and led me down the street.

11

er name was Brigit, since her mother, who some random man had planted his seed in back in the day, had been Irish. When it came to caresses, Brigit knew how to give and to receive.

As we lay in her bed after our first bout of lovemaking, she told me in a whisper that she'd left her mother, who made her living as a whore in London, the day she turned eleven and heard her mother negotiating over her with a sweaty Viking.

I didn't ask what she'd lived on during the years she spent roaming this war-torn land. I assumed she had been out tempting the same fates I had in the years after my father's death but before I met Winston. The difference was that I could rely on my strength and my skill with a weapon if stealing food turned out to be impossible. Obviously, though, she had her own methods of forcing men to comply with her wishes.

I slid my finger over her breasts, felt her warm hand on my stomach, and her damp breath at my ear as she whispered confidingly that I had turned out not to be the least of all the men she'd known.

I responded that as women went I had encountered few who possessed her abilities and asked her if I shouldn't be leaving.

She responded with the shake of her head, which I could just make out in the moonlight coming through the window. Her bed was in a room up under the roof in a post-and-plank building back behind Saint Edmund's church.

"But your husband?"

"He doesn't come here," she replied, her fingers encircling my wrist.

"He doesn't?" I raised myself up on my elbow and stared at her, lying there facing me with her hair flowing over her shoulders and her soft, inviting curves.

"Does it look like there's room here for two?" she asked, gesturing with her hand in response to my look of disbelief.

Well, I had seen smaller spaces house more than two people in my time, which I pointed out.

"Me, too," she snorted.

When she didn't elaborate, I asked about her husband. What kind of man was he and how had she met him?

When she revealed her sharp teeth in a smile, I understood that whatever she'd been up to since she fled from her mother, she'd certainly learned to control a man. As long as he was of the right makeup.

It had happened a little more than six months ago. At a market in a town whose name she'd forgotten. As usual she'd been wandering around hunting for the opportunity to acquire food for her next meal when her eyes fell on a hollow-cheeked old man struggling with a large piece of canvas that the wind was threatening to pull away from him. Without thinking more about it, she grabbed the flapping cloth and pulled it down so that the old man could tie his leather cord through the grommet and attach it to a pole to form one side of a marketplace stall with the canvas.

After thanking her grumpily, the old man reached for yet another piece of canvas, cursed the wind, and with a sour glance encouraged her to help him out again. Once the market stall was erected, she had set about arranging his wares without a word until they looked nice. Woolen goods, that's what he sold. Felt caps and sweaters, hosiery and trousers, woven cloth from Flanders and thick fabrics from the islands north of Scotland.

The whole time she was arranging things, the old man kept clearing his throat and coughing but had not said anything. Only once customers started flocking around did he push her aside and make it clear to her that he wanted to do the selling himself. Then she sat down in a corner and remained quiet, watching him make deals, and by nightfall she had realized two things: he was a shrewd businessman and he coughed like he was trying to spit out a lung.

Without a word, she started helping him pack up once the last customer had left, and although he gave her a sidelong glance, he didn't say anything and let her continue while he leaned heavily against one of the stall's poles. When she was done, he invited her to dinner at the nearest tavern and then left her without a word.

The following morning she was waiting for him and his mule-drawn cart. They walked together in silence the entire day on their way to the next market town, but that evening he did not invite her to dinner. The same thing happened the next day, but when they reached their destination three days later, she helped him set up his stall and take it down, and she ate her fill with him afterward.

Then three weeks passed without an offer for food, so she left him.

When she came back after five days, he lit up when she sat down on his cart and then he let her ride there. That evening he invited her to dinner again.

The next morning she stood silently next to the cart and when he passed her the canvas, she set it back down on the ground without a word.

It didn't take long after that for him to understand that if he wanted her help, it had its price.

"Marriage?" I asked. I'd been listening spellbound. She was a good storyteller.

I could hear as much as see her smile.

"He acknowledged me as his wife that very day."

"Why not just let him pay you for your work?"

"I do," she said, laughing loudly. "My payment is due when he runs out of time. When he keels over, I mean."

She must have noted my disbelief, because she said, *"Can a woman own anything?"*

Then I understood. A woman can't own anything within her marriage, but a widow owns her inheritance and whatever she can grow it into.

"And he leaves you alone?"

She chuckled. "He's been sleeping in his cart for years. I refused to do that, but I also made it clear that I don't see any reason to throw away any more money than absolutely necessary. So I always find the smallest room there is, and he's happy because he's saving money."

And that money, I realized, was being put aside for her inheritance.

"And if by 'leave me alone' you mean he doesn't demand his marital rights, well, that's true, mostly. But it does happen that he occasionally says ahem and something about my being his wife, and then I help him out as best I can. He's no spring chicken, so it usually takes most of a night to get him off. In return he's so grateful the next day, he lets me have whatever I point to."

I caressed her breast and whispered that she was too good to make do with an old man, which made her roll over onto her back and say that she wasn't ashamed of it, hadn't I realized that by now?

"There's no shortage of young men willing to make a young lady happy." Her hand slid down to my stomach. "The skill is in picking wisely, of course, but I know something about that from my earlier years. And if I get into a tight spot, of course I've planned for that."

"Planned for that?" I gasped for air as her hand encircled me.

"By helping him come to me this way about once a month." She giggled. "Can you imagine his pride if he ever got me with child?"

Her fingers and tongue inflamed me. I hadn't been with a woman in a long time, and I congratulated myself at having been in the right place at the right time.

12

nder a blue spring sky I walked through the narrow streets early the next morning toward the inn, the market and town waking up around me.

Smoke rose from the smokeholes in the roofs, and horses whinnied down by the river as they approached the water. Girls sang through open half doors, and the air smelled of porridge mixed with the malty scent of ale being heated in taverns and ale stands.

I greeted passersby, and I smiled at a boy with a prominent jaw who was struggling with an ale keg that was threatening to get away from him but which he gained control of at the last second. I drank in the crisp spring air in deep breaths and felt ready for whatever the day would bring.

Which was good because when I turned into the little square in front of the inn, I saw armed soldiers in front of it and heard angry voices from inside the half-open door.

The guards glared at me and stepped in my way, but they allowed me to proceed once I explained I was staying at the inn. I entered the tavern, where five men were in the middle of a major argument.

One of them was that scrawny beanpole who ran the place, Willibrord. Sigvald and Alwyn were next to him, their faces bright red. Reeve Turstan sat across from them wearing blue breeches with a gold hilted sword at his side. A flat-bellied man with an enormous rib cage was at his side, and judging by the silver rings that decorated his powerful upper arms, I thought him to be a trusted soldier.

Behind them I could just glimpse Winston, who hardly deigned to glance at me. He was leaning back on the bench, watching the loud men as he scooped porridge from a bowl in his lap. Seated across from him, Alfilda looked over her shoulder and gave me a jaunty smile. Then she tossed her head so that her hair fell over her shoulders and licked some honey off her horn spoon before dipping it into the bowl in front of her.

I stood quietly listening to the argument without getting much out of it. Turstan vehemently insisted that the farmers and the host tell him "where he is," and Sigvald crossly replied that as he had already told him, he had no idea.

The soldier with the silver rings glanced over at me, but he didn't say anything as I calmly crossed the room and sat down on the bench next to Winston and asked what was going on.

"Arnulf is gone," Winston said, calmly wiping his lips.

"He left? Where did he go?"

Winston shrugged and said, "No one knows. Turstan arrived a little while ago with a bunch of soldiers demanding access to the inn. Alfilda and I had just come down for breakfast when Willibrord answered the door and had to let them in. Reeve Turstan and his soldier demanded to speak to Arnulf, so Willibrord took them upstairs. But then they came back down again with the two farmers and there hasn't been a quiet moment since."

I looked around and spotted a grimy wench, held up my hand to her, and nodded when she held up a bowl.

"But Arnulf is here, isn't he?" I asked.

Winston shook his head.

The porridge was as good as the day before, the ale not too hot to drink but warm enough to chase the cold out of your body. And I was hungry, so I dug in while the argument raged on. As far as I could make out, Turstan accepted that the farmers had no idea where Arnulf was, but he refused to believe that they didn't know when he'd left the inn.

"Nor did we say that." Alwyn sounded tired, like a man who realized that no matter what he said, he wouldn't be believed. "He left the inn yesterday."

Turstan made an angry gesture with his hand and roared, "I'm not talking about yesterday."

Sigvald sounded equally tired when he chimed in, "But we are because we haven't seen him since then." Sigvald looked over at us. "Ask those guys over there."

Turstan glanced in our direction for the first time, and said, "You were with Arnulf at the court."

Winston nodded.

"But you didn't testify."

Winston stuck his spoon in his pocket and explained succinctly who we were—just that we were on our way to Saint Edmund's Town—and why we were with Arnulf. Then he cocked his head to the side and asked why Turstan wanted to talk to Arnulf.

Turstan studied him and glanced at me and Alfilda before he raised his eyebrows slightly and responded that he had some questions about the murder that had been committed the day before.

"The murder of Darwyn, son of Delwyn?" Winston asked.

Turstan nodded.

"Witnesses have testified under oath that Arnulf could not have committed that murder," Winston explained.

Turstan snorted haughtily.

Winston furrowed his brow and tugged on his nose without any other visible response to the thane's arrogant demeanor. Finally Winston looked up at Turstan and said, "Do you mean that if one man can perjure himself for a friend, a farmer's companions can do the same?"

"Is it your claim that Darwyn and Bardolf perjured themselves?" Turstan exclaimed, reddening with anger.

Winston stared Turstan in the eyes for a while, then cleared his throat and asked calmly if Turstan was claiming that he believed otherwise.

I noticed the ring-clad soldier jump to his feet, but Turstan didn't move at all. Finally Turstan shook his head slowly and said, "Are you claiming that farmers can't do the same?"

Now it was Winston's turn to shake his head. "The chance exists, but it's small."

"Oh?" Turstan evidently didn't agree.

"Two men can lie and keep it under wraps. In my experience, the more men who are in on a lie, the harder it is to keep hidden."

"But not impossible," Turstan said, biting his lip.

"No, not impossible."

"And have you seen this Arnulf?"

Winston shook his head. "Not since he left the tavern yesterday afternoon." He turned to look at me, and now it was my turn to shake my head.

"And," Winston continued, "my lady and I were sitting here until late last night without any sign of him."

Willibrord, who had stood by silently until now, took a step forward and said that he had locked the door before Winston and Alfilda went upstairs.

"And were these farmers back by then?" Turstan asked, staring hard at him.

Willibrord cleared his throat and replied, "They had been back for a while. Winston's company was the last to leave, and then I put the crossbar on the door."

So Alfilda and Winston had closed the place down with the coin makers.

Winston rubbed his chin and said, "Are you thinking the same thing I'm thinking, Reeve Turstan?"

There was a glint in Turstan's eye. Then he looked at his soldier and didn't say anything until the soldier nodded.

"That something happened to Arnulf the Farmer."

That thought had occurred to me ages ago, but had been supplanted by another: maybe he just went home, sick with grief at having been hoodwinked out of his silver?

Turstan turned to Alwyn and Sigvald and asked, "You're sure this Arnulf didn't sleep in the room last night?"

Sigvald was definitely scrawny, but when he stood up he radiated self-confidence.

"That's what I've been trying to convince you of for ages," Sigvald said.

"Should I send out the men?" the soldier asked, opening his mouth for the first time. His voice was deep and scratchy. My guess was that he'd shut down some other drinking establishment the previous night.

"He'll be found," Turstan said. "Until then, everyone must stay here."

Winston argued, "But there are men here who know him."

Turstan retorted, "And who could find him and warn him if they wanted."

Now it wasn't self-confidence but indignation oozing out of Sigvald's slender body.

"We have no reason to want anything other than to lead our friend safely here, so again, by our oaths, we repeat that he must be innocent," Sigvald said.

"All the same," Turstan said, brushing Sigvald off, "you'll stay here until we've found him."

"There are six men outside," Turstan told his soldier. "Leave two to guard the door so no one leaves without the host's word that they're not staying here." Out of consideration for Willibrord's right to profits he didn't order the door closed to thirsty or hungry tavern customers. "Have the other four go through the market and the town with a fine-toothed comb."

"My man knows Arnulf and has no stake in this case," Winston said with a glance at me. "He'd be happy to go along."

I shot an annoyed look at Winston. First of all, I'd been planning to get a little rest after the previous night's feats. Second, I didn't hear him volunteering his own services.

Turstan hesitated, then nodded.

"Stigand! You two go together," Turstan ordered.

With a sulky glance at Winston, I crossed the room and opened the door for Stigand, who indicated I should go first.

13

tigand was a man of few words. In clipped sentences he told the guards to find the man who had lost his case before the court the previous day.

"You all saw him?" he asked them.

They nodded, and two of them were curtly ordered to take up position outside the doors to the inn to carry out Turstan's orders. The other four were dispatched into town with a hand gesture.

Stigand stood quietly in the morning sun until a shiver ran through his body, like someone waking up from a dream, and he looked me over.

"You're carrying a sword," he pointed out.

"As are you." Stigand had a leather-hilted weapon hanging at his hip.

His brow furrowed but then immediately smoothed out again. Then he shrugged and said, "Let's go." ·

Silence didn't scare me. I was fond of it myself and had once pointed out to Alfilda that one of the reasons I welcomed her as Winston's woman was that now she was the object of his some-times suffocating torrent of words, which could drive me crazy when he wasn't busy with his artwork or investigating a case.

The market wasn't overly crowded yet, so early in the day. You could see down the alleys and streets, so if Arnulf suddenly showed up, we would spot him, not that I imagined that was an option. The man had surely—as I'd thought at the tavern—either headed home or had fallen victim to a nobleman's revenge, whether Delwyn had doled out the payback himself or left it to someone else. Therefore I didn't spend much time looking down streets. Nor did Stigand, who likely thought as I did.

Instead we looked under buckboards and behind counters and benches; we lifted up tent flaps, stepped into market stalls and small shops (despite their owners' protests), and peered into dark corners and behind sacks and barrels. We spent most of the late morning this way without running into anything other than a couple of drunk merchants, who were sleeping it off, and in one spot, a whore servicing a greasy tradesman, who just gave us a quick glance and proceeded to finish up with her.

Stigand and I hadn't exchanged many words during our survey of the market stalls, just a "look over there" or "I already checked that one," but we didn't get in each other's way at all.

Now I stopped at the sight of a wool merchant's stall.

The seller was skinny as a spear shaft, stooped, and bald apart from a greasy braid at the nape of his neck. His face was sharp, his skin like one of Winston's parchments after he'd stretched it on the frame, his cheeks hollow, his neck alarmingly thin, and his runny eyes deep set.

It was no surprise Brigit was expecting to inherit before too long.

She stood behind him, her eyes virtuously downcast, which was probably necessary since every single man nearby was openly ogling her. And for good reason. Her hair gleamed in the sun, and her full cheeks glowed. The curves of her breasts were visible beneath her blouse, because although she had demurely tossed a cape over herself, she let it hang open in the front. When she moved to lift a piece of cloth or hold up a tunic, she ran her hands down the front of her body, seemingly at random, emphasizing her curves.

I stepped over to the market stall, held up a cap to her, and asked what it would cost. With a virtuous curtsy, she replied that if I wanted to buy something, I should speak to her husband.

I glanced at the old man, who—between coughs—was working on convincing a corpulent matron of the quality of a piece of woven cloth. I leaned forward and whispered to Brigit, "Tonight?"

"Maybe," she said. She didn't look me in the eye until she'd turned and started folding a sweater.

Stigand cleared his throat behind me.

I waited. The old man increased his efforts to close the sale. Brigit placed the sweater in a stack of sweaters and then turned to me. She was still looking demurely at the ground.

"My husband will be ready to sell the hat to you momentarily."

Impatience made my throat constrict.

"Tonight?" I hissed as quietly as I could.

She responded with a shrug and then turned her back to me. I felt Stigand's hand on my arm and tugged firmly to pull myself free. Stigand was strong.

"We're carrying out the reeve's orders," he reminded me and pulled me along without further ado.

I stopped, dug in my heels, and leaned away from him, only to be tugged farther.

"Let go of me," I said, angrily slapping his hand where it grasped my arm.

He did as I asked and we walked side by side down the street while I tried to calm the flush in my face. After a minute he veered off into an ale tent. I followed, wondering if I should punch him, but realized that with the strength he'd demonstrated, I would be wise to refrain.

Soon we were sitting across from each other, each with a tankard. He raised his, drank, and set the tankard back down half-empty.

"Ah, that helped," he said.

I didn't respond, just drank, staring at the table in front of me.

"I don't think that Arnulf fellow is at the market," Stigand said.

I looked up and found him watching me calmly.

"He might have ridden back home to the village." It annoyed me to have to speak civilly to Stigand, but unless I wanted to fight him, I was going to have to swallow my pride.

"Perhaps he fled," Stigand said.

"Why would he have reason to do that? He didn't kill Darwyn," I said, shaking my head.

"According to his pals anyway," Stigand said.

"They're telling the truth," I said. "I'm convinced. As my master pointed out, it's hard to hide a lie among more than two men."

"Still, he could have run away."

"Why?" I asked, but then I understood. "Out of fear that Delwyn didn't care what the farmers said and was going to kill him simply out of anger at his son's death."

"It's been known to happen," Stigand said.

We drank for a bit while I pondered. Once our tankards were empty, we ordered two new ones, which we drained in silence.

"His horse!" I said, standing up. "Let's go down to the paddock and look."

Now that the market had picked up, it took a little while to get through. Just as we were passing the woolen ware stall, we had to stand still for a few moments until the crowds moved ahead. I glanced over and noticed Brigit standing as before, but her husband was sitting behind her enjoying a slab of pork.

I don't know if she noticed me looking or was just tired of standing around like a virtuous wife, but she looked up and stared at me. Then so quickly that I had to wonder if it had really happened, she winked, puckered her lips, and went right back to looking virtuous.

Stigand gave a rumbling laugh and said, "She's good, that one."

I didn't respond. Instead, I jabbed my shoulder into a stubborn, rough-looking Viking who was trying to push his way not past but through me. I thrust a fist into his soft belly at the same time and heard him gasp for air as he yielded. Once I squeezed by him, things were better.

My red gelding came running over when he saw me, snorting and nuzzling my hand, but was disappointed that I'd come empty-handed.

"Do you see it?" Stigand yelled. Then he burped loudly, causing a couple of the horses in the paddock to look up.

The gray mare was grazing peacefully next to Atheling, which said quite a bit about the mare's ability to assert herself.

"He didn't take his horse," I announced.

Stigand turned so that his back was to the wattle fence surrounding the paddock and burped again, although somewhat more discreetly this time. Then he jutted his chest out, took a deep breath, and exhaled with a sound like a bellows.

"Do you own land?" he asked.

I looked at him, confused, and then realized he was back to wondering why I carried a sword.

"Not currently," I said.

"Either you own land or you don't." He laughed his rumbling laugh. "Why do you carry the sword?"

My story was no secret; so many people knew it by now.

"My father lost his life at the Battle of Assandun along with my brother. All of my inheritance went to the Danes," I explained.

"The sword indicates that you think you're a thane."

I bit my lip. My hopes for my future, unlike what I'd just told him, were not common knowledge.

"I carry the sword so that I can protect my master, Winston the Illuminator."

Stigand raised his eyebrows, so I explained further, even though I thought that should have sufficed.

"He carries valuable items with him. An illuminator uses not only gold, but also other expensive materials to carry out his work."

Stigand was quiet. Maybe he believed me.

"And you? How many hamlets do you own?" I asked him.

He chuckled. "None. My father is still alive."

Ah, so he served the reeve while awaiting his inheritance. But it turned out I was wrong.

"And so is my older brother," he continued. "When my old man dies, my inheritance will be the sword I'm wearing."

I turned to look at him and detected a faint smile. We nodded to each other in mutual recognition that we both hoped that one day we would regain the right to claim we were thanes.

We stood next to each other, enjoying the sun's warmth. The horses grazed behind us, and we heard the sounds of swishing tails as they slapped at the buzzing flies. And then there was a new sound, a horse's worried whinny.

We turned and saw my red gelding all the way down by the river behind a large gorse bush. He stamped his front hooves, anxiously flung his head, and showed the whites of his eyes, before rearing and running away from the bush.

Leaving the fence behind us, we strode through the grass. A couple of horses had gone over to the bush, curious to see what had frightened the gelding, and now they too reared and whinnied and started galloping around the paddock, which made all the animals anxious, so it was like walking through a thunderstorm of hoofbeats.

We reached the gorse bush and walked around to the far side.

Stigand cocked his head and gave me a questioning look. I nodded.

We had found Arnulf.

Noses on the Trail

14

A lot had happened since Stigand and I bent over Arnulf's dead body.

He had been lying curled up on his side with his hand pressed to his right side, as if he wanted to stop the blood that was flowing out of him, but when we rolled him onto his back, we saw he'd been stabbed in several places.

Arnulf's collar was soaked with blood from a thin cut on the neck, the fingers of his left hand and right forearm had gashes, and when I opened his right hand, it was similarly cut up. His shirt was full of holes and bloody from a small stab wound below his breastbone.

I carefully placed my hand under the dead man's shoulder and lifted him long enough to see the grass beneath him, and then glanced at Stigand, who straightened up. He looked around the paddock as if whoever had committed the murder was waiting for us, which I told him was not the case.

"He's been lying here all night," I said.

Stigand's eyes widened a bit, curious at how I knew that.

"His clothes are still damp from the dew," I explained. "But his back is dry."

"The horse didn't find him until just now?"

I heard the skepticism in his voice and scanned the meadow. About thirty paces away from us, the grass had been trampled down into mud and sand leading all the way to the river.

"The horses have been drinking over there," I said.

He nodded. "So why did the red one come down here earlier?"

I pointed out that there was really no way for me to explain that. "Who knows why a horse thinks the way it does?" I peered across the river at the northern part of town. The buildings over there all faced away from the river.

Stigand noticed what I was looking at and said, "A few windows on this side would have been nice."

"Would it have helped, though?" I said with a shrug. "If the murder took place after sunset, it would have been dark over here."

He shook his head, which confused me until I realized he was right.

"It was a full moon," I said.

"But the buildings are so close together it's hard to believe anyone would have squeezed through those narrow side yards to stand and stare at the river. Oh well," he continued almost cheerfully, "it doesn't matter. We already know who did it."

I opened my mouth to correct him, but decided against it. Instead I asked if he wanted to inform the reeve.

He bit his lip and glanced back over at our part of town. He spotted two of his men and shouted for them to come over. They obeyed, eyes widening at the sight of the body, but silently took up position, promising to guard the body until we had more specific orders.

We parted at the ale stand, and I continued on to the inn, where the door was still under guard. I found Winston and Alfilda in the tavern engaged in idle conversation with the two coin makers, who were listening raptly to Winston.

I walked up behind the coin makers, facing my companions, and waited for Winston to finish his speech.

Alfilda looked at me first. Her eyes looked a little glazed over from boredom. Then she noticed the fire in my eyes and put her hand on Winston's arm. Winston glanced at her with regret and continued pontificating, but when he saw my expression he paused. The coin smiths turned around and peered at me with curiosity.

"Master Erwin," Winston said standing up. "And you, Harold. You'll have to excuse us."

Their faces fell, and they sat for a moment, at a loss for what to do. Then Erwin stood up, bowed aloofly to Alfilda and walked stiffly toward the door followed by his journeyman.

The door banged shut behind them.

"You found Arnulf?" Winston asked.

"Yes."

"Dead?" Alfilda asked.

"Yes," I said again, and explained that Stigand had informed the reeve.

"Do tell," said Winston, sitting back down and gesturing to the bench across from him.

They both listened to my account and then sat for a while, Winston with his hands folded on the table in front of him, Alfilda with one of her hands on his arm again.

"So Stigand thinks Delwyn took his revenge?"

I confirmed this.

"And what do you think?" Winston asked.

I grinned at them. "I think words mean a lot right now. Untruthful as well as truthful. I believe Delwyn will swear himself free in this case."

"And will he be swearing truthfully?" Winston asked with a penetrating stare.

"In my opinion, yes."

Winston was quiet again. Then he looked me in the eye. "Do we owe Arnulf anything?"

Before I could respond, Alfilda said quietly, "He did show us hospitality."

"And," I said just as quietly, "that would give us an excuse for remaining in town for a while."

"So we're going to—" Winston didn't get any further than that.

The door to the tavern opened and Reeve Turstan's expensively dressed form entered. He headed straight for our table.

"You!" He was pointing at me. "You led Stigand to the body."

I saw Stigand glance at me from behind Turstan.

"No," I replied.

"So my man is lying?" Turstan said, glaring at me.

"That depends on what he said." I leaned back on the bench forgetting there was no backrest, so I must have looked downright silly as I jerked back upright trying to regain my balance.

"He told me you led him to the paddock and then to the body."

I looked over Turstan's shoulder at Stigand and shook my head sadly. "If he used the word 'led,' then, yes, he's lying."

I saw Stigand blink, and I understood. That was the reeve's word choice, not his. I turned back to Turstan. "As I'm sure Stigand told you, it occurred to us that Arnulf might have fled, fearing Delwyn's thirst for revenge. We both thought of it at the same time, and we walked down to the paddock to see if Arnulf's horse was there. My horse led us to the body. Hopefully you won't hold that against me."

Reeve Turstan didn't seem to be in a joking mood. "The farmer had no reason to fear Delwyn."

Now Winston joined in. "Surely farmers always think they have reason to fear thanes."

"Farmers think a lot of things. Law and order prevail in my town." Turstan flung his hand up in a gesture of annoyance, and I thought it was wisest not to mention that the previous day's court session had demonstrated that law and order did not always ensure justice.

"If I might ask?" Winston is always his most polite when he most wants to be impolite. "What does Delwyn himself say?"

"I have sent men for him." Turstan heard footsteps on the stairs and looked up. Our traveling companions were coming downstairs with Sigvald in the lead. There was no knowing whether they were drawn by the noise or hunger due to the approaching dinner hour. They stopped short when they saw the reeve.

"You found him!" Alwyn exclaimed.

Before anyone could respond, the front door flung open again, and Delwyn walked in with three soldiers. It was starting to get crowded in this tavern.

"You had me summoned." Delwyn didn't deign to look at the rest of us, addressing only the reeve.

"I wanted to inform you that Arnulf the Farmer has been found dead."

Delwyn's eyes widened. "Dead? Killed?"

"Yes," Turstan said.

"Who did it?" Delwyn glanced at the rest of us.

"That we don't know," Turstan said, biting his lip.

Delwyn looked at Winston and said, "You asserted yesterday that Arnulf hadn't killed my son. Do you still claim this?"

Winston nodded.

"Do you think I believed you?"

"Yes." There was no hesitation in Winston's voice.

Delwyn looked back at Turstan and growled, "Shall I swear to my innocence?"

Turstan opened his mouth, but Winston spoke first. "That's hardly necessary."

Everyone looked at Winston, who gestured to me and said, "Tell them where you found Arnulf."

I repeated my account and looked at Stigand as I finished and asked, "Do you agree?"

He cleared his throat and said yes.

"And my oath, which I will gladly give, isn't necessary, because . . . ?" Delwyn began, his brow furrowed.

"Because Arnulf was stabbed with a knife." I strove to speak as objectively as possible. Everyone was staring at me now, so I continued. "The stab wound in his chest was too narrow to have been caused by a sword or a spear. The cut in his neck was thin, almost delicate. At any rate, it wasn't from a sword. It came from Arnulf pulling away from a swinging knife blade."

I nodded to Delwyn and his men and explained, "You carry swords and spears. Your daggers are double-edged and wide. Arnulf was defending himself against a single-edged knife."

The tavern was completely silent. If I were a bard, I would have been proud of my ability to captivate my audience.

"Arnulf grabbed with his left hand to fend off the blow," I explained. "Only his fingers were cut by the blade. If the knife had been double-edged, he would have had wounds in his palm as well. He had that in his right hand since his palm was facing the knife he was fending off. The fingers of his right hand, however, had no wounds."

I stopped.

Delwyn was the first to speak. "My son was also stabbed with a knife." Then he looked at the farmers. All farmers carry a single-edged knife.

I cleared my throat and continued. "That occurred to us as well, Delwyn. But two things suggest the farmers didn't do it: Why would they kill your son? His lie did not harm them. It only harmed Arnulf. And why go to Thetford to kill *Arnulf*? Surely they had better opportunities to do that at home."

Silence fell over the tavern. Everyone seemed to be considering what I'd said.

When Delwyn finally spoke, he was still growling. "You and your master can certainly think. Do you believe there's any connection between the two murders?"

I let Winston respond. "It seems obvious that there isn't."

Delwyn turned to look at Turstan and said, "Thank you for not demanding my oath. But my son perjured himself, and if I have to live with that shame, I would feel better at least knowing his murderer had been found."

He looked me in the eye and said, "Will you clear up the murder of my son?"

"I'm not my own man."

Delwyn turned to Winston, who nodded. "We will get to the bottom of both killings if we can."

It was drizzling and although the evening was mild, I shivered in my wet clothes. The red gelding stretched beneath me, seeming glad to be allowed to move, and the trail lay open ahead of me, so I maintained a good speed and would reach my destination before dark.

Winston had sent me north, back toward where the case had begun. I would have preferred to stay in Thetford doing my part to solve the mystery. However, Winston felt that in town we would bump into Turstan no matter where we turned, and since Winston was the one who paid my wages, the decision was his.

And he was probably right, my master.

Which was why I was now riding north toward Arnulf's farm instead of resting between Brigit's inviting thighs.

15

othing is ever as straightforward as one would like, however.

Turstan had pulled Delwyn away from the rest of us by his arm, and into the shadows up against the wall. We couldn't hear everything they said, but Turstan was obviously expressing his dissatisfaction.

In his opinion the farmers should have been permitted to swear their innocence of the killing and, if they consented, then the murderer should be sought "among the other farmers whose women your son raped." We had all heard that bit.

Delwyn had twisted his arm free from Turstan's grasp, looked over his shoulder at Winston, and said, "When you have the murderer, bring him to me."

Winston nodded.

Turstan flung up his hands, giving up. He looked at the farmers who stood in silence by the stairs, watching the angry nobleman with wide eyes.

"You lot stay here," Turstan instructed the farmers.

"Our business in Thetford is done," Sigvald said, looking up suddenly.

"But you will remain here!" Turstan spat. "In my experience, men are killed by people they know, people who are close to them. Let the damn illuminator look elsewhere for the murderer. When he eventually admits the folly of his investigation, then you can leave." He paused and then added, "Once you've sworn to your innocence."

"But . . ." Sigvald said, pushed to the front of his group by the others, "we can't sit around here in the tavern, waiting for days."

Turstan twisted his lips into a stiff smile and conceded, "You can go as far as the gates."

It was an unreasonable order, that farmers should sit trapped in a town when the spring farmwork was only half-done in their fields and meadows. But Turstan did not give them the opportunity to argue. He turned his back on them and walked toward the door, his legs stiff. Then he waited for Stigand to open it for him and stepped out, not like a man leaving a tavern, but like one entering his hall.

Delwyn hesitated a little, then agreed, and exited, followed by his three soldiers.

It was quiet. Winston tugged on his nose. Alfilda's eyes were on the farmers, who hadn't moved since coming downstairs. I was contemplating how many farm wenches Darwyn had raped.

"Can any of you tell me anything that could simplify my task?" Winston eyed the five farmers. Herward snorted so his mustache quivered. Alwyn scratched his crotch. Bjarne ran his fingers through his beard. Sigvald pulled his knife in and out of his sheath until he suddenly realized what he was doing, stuck it back in, and let go of the handle. His son looked at the floor, biting his lip.

"Well?" Winston asked patiently.

They shook their heads.

Winston let me eat before sending me off. At Alfilda's suggestion that we find a place to eat where we could sit by ourselves, we left the tavern and found an ale tent at the edge of the market. We sat down at the farthest table, out where the meadow began its drop down to the river.

"Turstan is right, isn't he?" Alfilda asked, biting into a piece of rye bread so sour that she made a face and set it down again. Instead she took a bite of one of the boiled pork neck bones, which had been placed before us in a dish, bit off a good-sized chunk of it and licked the drippings off her fingers before she pushed the clay dish over to me.

"About what?" Winston asked, drinking from the birch burl cup.

"Killing is often done by someone who knows the victim," Alfilda said, sucking on a finger. "Murder, I mean. Not killing in battle or a barroom brawl."

And of course she—and Turstan—were right about that. I have yet to see a man be murdered by a stranger. A stranger might kill someone by accident, but murder takes place between people who know each other.

"And yet Turstan didn't make the farmers swear right then and there," I pointed out. The meat was tender, and I sucked a neck bone clean.

Winston smiled fleetingly, then spoke. "He emphasized that since Delwyn chose to go his own way in seeking revenge, that's the path the reeve has to follow." He paused to take a bite of the meat, then licked the grease from the corners of his mouth before continuing. "Delwyn chose us. Turstan interprets that to mean that *he* no longer needs to solve the mystery."

"Yeah," I said, spitting out a thyme stem. "But then why not let the farmers go home?"

Alfilda was the one who responded. "Turstan doesn't think we can solve the case."

"Exactly," Winston said, looking at me. "And hadn't you just told him and everyone else that we don't think one of the farmers killed both victims? In other words, he's hoping we'll fail. Then he can take over the case and show that one of the farmers is the murderer."

"I was right when I said they weren't, wasn't I?"

"I think so," said Alfilda. "For the reasons you stated. None of them had any score to settle with Darwyn, and each of them had had countless opportunities to murder Arnulf back at home."

"Darwyn could have done something to one of their women," I said, thinking about what Turstan had said.

Winston and Alfilda nodded.

"I thought that, too." Winston spat out a piece of cartilage. "That's why you're going to ride to the village."

I looked at him in surprise.

"For a few reasons," Winston continued. "Here in town, the reeve will undoubtedly try to impede our investigation. Which he can do as easily as he can scratch his own ass. So let's make sure there's no overlooked reason for murder back where the case began. Let's make sure that Darwyn was the only one Arnulf had a case against. Once we're sure of that, we can meet the good reeve and point out that the case needs to be solved here in town. If necessary, we'll convince the farmers to swear to their innocence and thereby force Turstan to help us, or at least to remove the impediments from our path."

"Wouldn't it be easier to just have them swear their innocence now?" I asked.

"It would"—Winston acknowledged with his familiar knowing smile—"but you're forgetting one thing."

"The reeve won't accept it," Alfilda said.

The dish was empty, and I pushed it to the middle of the table, let Alfilda fill my cup from the pitcher, and eyed Winston.

"Anything else?" I asked.

"What's Arnulf's wife's name?" Winston asked.

Alfilda and I stared blankly at each other.

"I really have no idea," I finally admitted.

Winston leaned forward, looking expectantly at Alfilda, who shook her head.

"I don't remember it either," she said.

"Because no one ever told us her name," Winston said. "That's no way for a farmer to treat his wife. And not just any farmer, a well-to-do farmer so rich that all three of us thought he was a thane. He didn't invite her to join us at the table even though there were guests for dinner. He didn't introduce her or let her meet Alfilda, which is customary when a woman comes to visit. He was greedy and obsessed with money as we've seen, but also obviously stingy in other ways toward his wife."

Winston paused and drained his cup.

"Am I the only one of us who would be interested in knowing how a wife who has been treated that way by her husband reacts when she receives the news that he's been murdered?"

16

I reached Arnulf's farm before nightfall. The ride sat like lead in my thighs as I arduously swung my leg over and out of the saddle. Although the drizzle had stopped a while ago, I still felt damp and cold, and I was looking forward to a blazing fire and a tankard of warm ale.

It was quiet. Not even the sound of a dog.

My red gelding neighed and a shiver ran down his flank. I put a hand on his shoulder, drew my sword, and peered around, alert. I had never known a village to be this quiet. As a rule, you were greeted by dogs barking as soon as you approached the outer fence; barks alerted the menfolk and sent the women and children indoors until the men made sure that the traveler came in peace.

I looked up. The moon hadn't risen yet, but the sky was still lit by the dusk. A shadow swooped in from the right, and I heard the rustle of a nightjar, so I immediately raised my left hand with my pinkie and ring finger outstretched the way Harding had taught me to ward off the evil of the wretched dead, doomed to fly in the form of the bird.

I sniffed. The sour odor of smoke hit my nostrils—not the smell of burning, I determined, but the smell of wet firewood and damp peat. A glance at the roofline revealed gray smoke rising from the smokehole. I turned to look at the other two farms in the village and saw white smoke rising. I suppose Arnulf figured his wife, slaves, and servants could make do without dry wood for a proper fire when he was away.

With my sword at the ready, I walked around behind my horse, who stood stock-still. I peered around from building to building without seeing anything suspicious. Then I walked up to the door, and rapped on it with my sword hilt.

There was no discernable sound from inside.

Once again I scanned the area without spotting anything that looked out of place and then hammered my hilt on the door again.

It took a while, but then it opened a crack to me.

"I'm Halfdan bearing a message for the wife of Arnulf the Farmer."

The words were hardly out before the door was shut in my face. I stared at its solid timbers in outrage, shivered grumpily in my wet clothes, and then heard the gelding nicker. When I turned around, I swore a grumbling curse at the sight of four men behind me. Why I hadn't heard them, I had no idea. They were way too close to me.

The one on my left lowered his sword, which caused the rest to slowly follow suit, but from their hesitation, I had already determined that I was not facing soldiers. So I lunged at them with a bellow, feinting at their leader with my sword, but allowing the blade to drop so that it slid in below his spear shaft, which I was then able to knock out of his hand.

The other three jumped back in fear, but since I had determined these were men from the two other farms in the village, I lowered my sword and addressed their spearless leader.

"You heard me. I'm Halfdan and I have business with Arnulf's wife."

He opened his mouth, swallowed, and then croaked that she was in the hall behind me.

"Mists of Hel, don't you think I already know that?" I resheathed my sword with exaggerated drama. "Call in there and make them open up."

He moistened his lips with his fleshy tongue. He cleared his throat and then yelled in a voice that I suppose he meant to sound commanding that they should open up since he had made sure I came in peace.

I grinned at him, feeling superior, and then saw the door open. First just a crack, then far enough that I could squeeze my way in.

It was very dark inside. The hearth glowed gray in the middle of the hall and confirmed my thought that the fire was being fed with bad wood and damp peat. I could make out a few silhouettes behind it, but the woman of the house did not come around the fire to bid me welcome.

I walked toward the embers, stopped a few paces away from them, and demanded that the fire be fed so that I could see who I was talking to.

My words were met with silence and then I heard a faint "Do it," followed by footsteps. I stood in silence for a few minutes, and then heard footsteps again. The fire was fed with a bundle of twigs and flared up. Then the flames subsided again as a few unsplit logs were placed on top, but soon they were burning with a quiet gleam that lit the middle of the hall.

I looked at Arnulf's wife for the first time. During our visit she had mostly stayed among the slaves and servants and only been with us briefly when she had ale brought out to the other farmers. She was a strong-looking woman with solid arms and a neck that could have fit on a bull calf. Her face was strangely narrow for such a muscular woman. She had pleasant features and smooth skin. She wore her blonde hair up and her blue eyes were bright.

I looked at the slave girl by her side. She was as pretty as she had been the first time I saw her, clean, with nice, albeit worn, clothes. She seemed unafraid, looking directly at me, her gray eyes containing a twinkle of mild challenge, as if she wanted me to question why a slave wench was being so free. In actuality, that mystery didn't concern me.

I bowed my head to the lady of the house and waited until she had returned my greeting.

"I'm Halfdan, and I bring news from Thetford," I announced.

I suppose she'd guessed that much. I couldn't say whether she'd also guessed that it was bad news, but her response to my next statement surprised me.

"Bad news," I said, softening my tone. "Arnulf is dead."

Her face, which was actually lovely, winced. From grief, I thought, before I saw the glint in her eyes. Relief or outright joy glimmered at me. What she did next took me so aback that my jaw actually dropped.

Arnulf's widow turned and embraced the slave girl, who then buried her face in the woman's ample bosom. They stood like that for a while, then let go of each other and turned to me. They both looked jubilant.

"Dead, you say," the widow said, holding out her hand to the slave girl, who grasped it.

I nodded, speechless. Then I pulled myself together.

"Murdered."

The woman's eyes widened a bit, otherwise her expression didn't change. Nor did the joy she had been radiating since hearing my news.

"And his case?" Her voice was casual.

Again I stood mute with surprise.

"Did he win it?" she inquired.

I shook my head, cleared my throat, and replied, "No. Darwyn had his own witness."

"He must have been crushed," the widow said, smiling broadly now.

I tried to catch the slave girl's eye. I succeeded and read the same gloating pleasure in it as in the widow's face.

"He . . . wasn't happy about it," I said.

"We can imagine," the slave girl said, opening her mouth for the first time. She had a pleasant voice.

"Mistress," I said, rubbing the back of my head in consternation. "Did you hear what I said?"

"Arnulf is dead," she said, nodding. "Murdered. Yes, I heard."

She suddenly turned and yelled through the hall. "This is my farm now and my hall. Fetch more wood and torches. Let's have some ale and food for the man who brought us these tidings!"

As I stood there, still flummoxed, there was a commotion in the hall. A slave brought over trestles, which had been by the bench along the wall, and placed planks on top to form a table. The slaves brought pitchers of ale, tankards, dishes of cold roast meat, a basket of bread, and a clay cask surrounded by small cups.

I grabbed a slave's arm as he passed and instructed him to look after my gelding, which didn't take him long, because he stepped back into the hall again soon after.

"Sit," the widow said, gesturing invitingly with her hand. I sat down silently on the bench, where I was soon joined by two of the farmhands, who remained silent, as if they had lost the power of speech.

The lady of the house pushed a chair without armrests up to the table across from me and signaled to the slave girl, who grabbed a stool and sat down beside her mistress without further ado.

The farm girls sat down at the short ends of the table with the slaves who had brought everything in.

The lady of the house stood up, took a tankard, filled it, and handed it to me before she poured ale into several more tankards, which were pushed across to the farmhands and slaves. Finally she poured mead from the clay cask into the small cups, which she placed in front of the girls and the slave wench.

When everyone had a full cup, she raised her own and drank to us. First to me, looking me in the eye, then the others. We raised our glasses back to her, and then I set down my tankard. As I looked around the table, I thought I was beginning to understand.

"My lady, I've given you my name. Might I know yours?"

"Gertrude Arnul . . ." She paused. "I'm the widow Gertrude."

I looked over at her slave and asked, "And you?"

"Rowena." The girl revealed an astonishingly complete mouthful of teeth.

One of the men pushed a bread basket toward me. I gratefully accepted it and a slice of pork, but held off on biting into the food.

"In addition to your husband, another man also lost his life in Thetford," I said, then paused until I had the woman's full attention. I briefly recounted the Hundred Court and the subsequent murder of Darwyn, to which she listened calmly.

I let my words sink in before I summarized. "Two men have been killed, one of them your own husband. But you don't seem all that sorrowful, Lady Gertrude."

"Sorrowful?" she said with a smile. "Sorrowful at the loss of the most tightfisted man who ever suckled a woman? The greediest farmer in all of East Anglia? A man who begrudged us food, but gladly lavished hospitality on strangers, so they would ride off and spread the word about that friendly farmer Arnulf? Who counted every fire log, every hunk of peat, every bundle of twigs before he left for the court to go collect the fine for an injustice he should have avenged on his own? No, Halfdan, I will never feel sorrow for him."

She paused and looked around the hall, which was now lit by the fire and torches.

"I will feel nothing but joy that everything he squirreled away will now provide for me in my widowhood."

I bit into the food. The meat was nicely stewed and fatty and the bread flavorful. I guessed that both came from the chest of things awaiting the master of the house's return. The wench across from me wasn't eating, but had drunk her cup of mead and now sat quietly, smiling, as if she had a secret that would soon be revealed to everyone.

"Your master chose not to avenge you." I couldn't forget what I'd come to sniff around for.

She looked me placidly in the eye, but a shadow fell over her face.

"Arnulf valued silver over justice," the slave girl said.

I nodded and asked, "And that made you mad?"

"Mad?" she replied with a look of scorn. "Slaves don't feel mad. There's no point."

Before I could respond, I heard the faint sound of hoofbeats. I looked around but seemed to be the only one who'd heard them. I let my left hand fall, grabbing the hilt of my sword and making sure it slid easily in its sheath.

We ate and drank in silence, and then someone pounded on the door.

Without a word, I stood up, put a finger to my lips and then pointed to one of the farmhands, who got up and walked over to the door.

"Wait," I said, drawing my sword and taking up position to the left of the doorway so that the door would open away from me. Then I gave a go-ahead gesture and stood completely still as the farmhand swung the solid door open.

I let the man come all the way into the hall before I stepped in behind him, moved my sword to his throat, and instructed him to stand completely still.

He obeyed. One glance showed that he did not carry a sword. He must have left his spear outside.

Over his shoulder I saw Rowena and Gertrude get up.

"Turn around. Slowly!" I ordered.

He obeyed and I found myself staring into Sigurd's frightened face.

17

he boy was exhausted from the ride—it showed in the deep furrows at the corners of his mouth, the gray glint to his skin, and his weather-beaten, matte eyes.

I also saw fear in his eyes. Not just fear at having been met with shining steel but also, undoubtedly, from the horror that comes from riding alone in the dark. Highwaymen can lurk behind any bush and around every bend in the path, and a lone rider is easy picking for scoundrels. Riding in the dark, it was often said, also brought danger from trolls and other supernatural, subterranean beings that lie in wait—beings against whom no sword could provide protection.

Yet he'd gone off into the dark all the same, ignoring the reeve's orders to remain in town. He had ridden through the darkness, which contained the risk of attack from ghouls as well as from others who might travel under the cloak of invisibility when it suited them.

Behind the boy's shoulder, I saw Rowena, and I had an inkling about the reason for his bravery.

"Well met, Sigurd son of Sigvald." I lowered my sword and stuck it back in its sheath. "You disobeyed the reeve's orders."

He gulped, staring at me. He looked like he was struggling with all his might not to look at the slave wench.

"He was pretty clear about his instructions, I think," I pointed out.

"I . . . I . . ."

"Yes?" I encouraged him.

"We thought we owed it to Gertrude to bring her the news of her husband's death." He was still gray, but there was some life in his eyes.

"And so they selected you to ride back." I nodded at him in recognition. "How kind of Turstan to grant you permission."

His mouth trembled and the strength left him so that he *had* to turn to Rowena, who was watching him wide-eyed.

"Look at me," I commanded. I know how to speak like someone who expects to be obeyed, which Harding always said was the prerequisite for anyone actually obeying you. "What is the penalty for disobeying the reeve's orders?" I didn't think it would be much. A fine maybe, but I wanted to put some fear into the man cub and continued, "Is he a harsh man, Turstan? Does he use the noose against farmers who cross him?"

We both heard the little yelp from Rowena, but we continued our staring match, and I did not look away first. Now I had him where I wanted him, so it was time to give him what he'd come for.

I looked at Gertrude and said, "Sigurd has ridden far and is tired and hungry."

Soon we were seated at the benches again. Rowena had squeezed in next to Sigurd, and while he hungrily shoveled in the food, she rested her hand on his arm and watched his face.

I let him eat his fill. I swallowed my ale and contemplated how to approach the case. By the time he was mopping up the last bits with a crust of bread, I had decided, but I sat in silence for a moment longer watching Rowena, who looked back at me nervously while her hand slowly slid down Sigurd's arm and found his hand.

"And here I was thinking you were cautious." I turned to Gertrude and explained, "As we rode away the other day, Sigurd was turning around in the saddle the whole time, looking back where we'd come from. Of course I thought he was making sure no highwaymen were following us, but it turns out robbers weren't what he was actually looking for."

I'll be darned if I didn't see the little slave wench out of the corner of my eye. She looked pleased.

"Was Arnulf aware of this?"

Gertrude said, "Arnulf knew all about it. Those two haven't been able to take their eyes off each other for several years."

She fell silent. She had just revealed to me that Darwyn's rape had affected someone beside Rowena.

I let that rest.

"But Arnulf was opposed to the match?" I asked.

Now Sigurd apparently felt it was up to him, as a man, to explain to me how everything fit together. "I asked to buy Rowena's freedom a year ago."

"And Arnulf set the price high," I said, able to guess what Arnulf would say to that.

"Arnulf . . ." Sigurd paused.

"Arnulf saw an opportunity to get some money out of Sigurd," Gertrude said, sounding almost apologetic. Then her voice changed and she continued snidely, "As in every other matter, he let his hunger for silver be his guide."

I dropped the subject and addressed Sigurd again. "You could hardly afford to buy her freedom yourself. What did your father think about this?"

"He . . ." Sigurd suddenly squeezed Rowena's hand. "He refused to pay more than the usual price for a slave girl."

I looked at Rowena and then Sigurd, whose face had finally regained some color. Young people always find a way out when the road ahead is blocked, but before I managed to ask the question, I realized why these two hadn't used it.

"And what did he threaten if you bedded her?"

Was that a blush I saw?

Gertrude responded, "Arnulf made it clear that any child would be born into slavery and would therefore belong to him."

I had no doubt Arnulf would have sold an infant, and not just for the sake of the silver.

"And," the mistress of the house continued, "he would take the case to court for the rape of a slave girl."

I didn't know the going price for a slave among the East Anglians, but I remembered that Arnulf had said the fine for raping a slave wench was sixty-five shillings, with additional compensation for her maidenhead. That was the fine Darwyn had sworn himself free of, and it might have been higher than the price Sigurd had been quoted for the wench.

I turned back to Sigurd and asked, "What about your father? Was the amount of silver required to buy her freedom your father's only objection to your having Rowena?"

This time Rowena was the only one who blushed. In anger this time, I thought.

"Not every farmer would welcome a slave wench as a daughter-in-law," I pointed out.

Sigurd fidgeted uneasily in his seat, but it was Gertrude who responded. "Welcome or not, he refused to pay too high a price. Especially," she stammered, "after Rowena was assaulted."

And lost some of her value, both as a slave and a daughter-in-law.

"There were no consequences from the rape?" I asked, looking at Rowena.

"No," she bowed her head in shame.

So the crime had resulted only in the loss of her maidenhead.

I bit my lip. Did they think I was too dumb to see that there was something they weren't saying? I chose to let it go—for now.

Instead I said, "The day before yesterday, after the court case, when Arnulf said that no pact or agreement could persist after the court's ruling, you went pale as a corpse. I thought you shared Arnulf's anger at the injustice that had been done. But that wasn't it, was it?"

Sigurd looked from Rowena to Gertrude, moistened his lips, and shook his head.

"Arnulf had promised that after Darwyn had paid the fine, I could buy Rowena's freedom for the standard price."

"And he broke that promise," I surmised. "Did you talk to him after that?"

Sigurd hesitated. Then he nodded.

"When Arnulf left the tavern, my father and I followed him."

So young Sigurd still needed his father's support. I couldn't begrudge him that.

"And?"

"He insisted on his inflated price," he said, shaking his head.

"And?" I repeated.

He looked at me blankly.

"So you followed him and stabbed him to death," I provided.

"No," he leapt up so that the bench tipped over and Rowena with it. He reached down for her in confusion and after he pulled her to her feet, he clutched her to him and pulled her down onto the now-righted bench.

"I didn't," he whispered into her hair.

"Of course not," she stroked his hair soothingly and kissed him on the cheek. "You're not a murderer."

Not being in love with him, I was not as sure as she about that.

Winston had sent me here to find out if the murders might have stemmed from something that happened in the village, and here I sat with a man who had more than good reason to kill *both* Darwyn and Arnulf.

"You're coming back to Thetford with me tomorrow," I told him.

Sigurd looked at me in terror, but neither his fear nor the look the slave wench gave me helped. I had to bring him to Winston so that, together, the two of us might wade through the lies.

"You have a choice," I said sternly. "You can come with me of your own free will and give me your word here and now that you will do so, or I'll bring you to town bound with rope and twine."

"You wouldn't do that," Rowena said, looking at me with contempt.

They didn't even have a chance to blink. In one motion I was up on my feet with my sword drawn. I hammered my weapon down into the table so that it gouged into the wood.

"Wouldn't I?" I asked coldly, calmly staring into their horrified faces.

"You," I growled across the hall to a slave, who regarded me with a trembling mouth. "Bring me some rope. Now!"

Rowena's lips quivered. She stepped in front of her boyfriend, but backed down when I lunged slightly with my sword.

"There is, of course, a third option," I hissed bitingly. "I could deliver a dead murderer to Reeve Turstan."

"I'm not a murderer!" Sigurd's voice was both defiant and on the verge of tears.

"You're not? I suspect the reeve will wonder why you ran away, then, despite his explicit order not to leave the inn."

"I'll go with you tomorrow," Sigurd said.

"Give me your word." I was still pointing the tip of my sword at them.

Sigurd straightened up and held out his hand to me.

"You have my word. I will accompany you to Thetford tomorrow."

And there you have it. That's what a woman will do to a man.

"Good." I sheathed my blade. "In return, I will try to get you into town without the reeve discovering you left."

Gertrude, Sigurd, and Rowena all stared at me blankly.

"Why?" Rowena asked, uncomprehending.

"It just may be that I'm not all that wild about letting pompous thanes order me around," I said with a smile.

Of course the truth was that I wanted Winston to have a chance to question the boy, but my lie accomplished what I'd hoped it would: they were farmers and unwilling to think anything good of a thane. My little lie signaled to them that I shared their opinion, thereby making me one of them.

Almost. I could see in Rowena's eyes that she remembered it was my nobleman's sword that had forced them to comply.

"Now go." I waved them away with my hand. "You have a night before we ride."

Rowena looked to Gertrude for permission, and when Gertrude nodded her consent, Rowena pulled her boyfriend behind her up the ladder to the alcove under the rafters, which she shared with the other girls and slave wenches. The girls and wenches, in turn, all sat down on the benches that ran along the sides of the hall.

"So you're giving them one night," I said, smiling at Gertrude, who looked back at me with a weighty expression.

"I'll give them all the nights they want. Sigurd didn't kill Darwyn or Arnulf."

I didn't say anything. I was sure they were lying about something.

Winston would have to help me untangle that lie once we had the boy alone without his girlfriend, from whom he clearly took his strength.

"It's a shabby man who doesn't want to avenge the rape of his girlfriend," I said, looking across the table at the mistress of the house.

"Sigurd is not a shabby man." Her whole face blushed. "But he does not go against his father's wishes."

"His father prevented him from taking revenge?" I asked.

"His father knows what happens when a farmer kills the son of a thane."

As did I. The whole village would have been nothing more than charred ruins.

"So they were counting on the Hundred Court?"

She nodded.

"Like Arnulf, they trusted that the court would give Rowena her redress."

But the court hadn't. And Gertrude had just said that Sigurd's father had kept Sigurd from taking action on his own in the hopes that the court would side with them.

When the court ruled unjustly, that freed Sigurd to act.

18

slept heavily that night. The ride had taken its toll on me, and Brigit hadn't given me much time to sleep the night before. Brigit. I sent a thought her way before sleep overcame me, and when I woke early in the morning, it was from a dream about her voluptuous body.

The hall was silent. I heard sleep sounds from the benches, but for me, who had sometimes shared a room and even a bed with Winston's deafening snores, these noises were like mere puffs of breeze through the heather.

The light in the hall was dim. The fire had burned itself out overnight, and a slave must have put out the torches after he came back in from seeing to Sigurd's horse.

I glanced over at the ladder for the alcove, which I'd removed and laid down on the floor before I turned in. It was still down, so I felt confident that Sigurd hadn't used the cover of night to sneak away.

Which I hadn't seriously expected him to do. There was someone to keep him here. All the same, I figured it was wisest to take precautions.

From outside the window over my bed I heard a starling singing. Dust motes floated in the rays of sunlight. I folded my hands behind my head and stared into the air.

Winston had asked if he was the only one who wondered how Arnulf's widow would take the news of his death. I had also wondered as I rode here the day before.

And I had been surprised.

I had been expecting confusion. I thought she'd be cast adrift at having been left behind by a power-hungry husband, that she'd be worried about all the decisions she would face.

I had not anticipated Gertrude's undisguised joy.

Nor the ease with which she would start doling out orders.

My thoughts turned to Sigurd. I had at first taken him for a naïve boy, but I now knew that he had restrained his own desire for vengeance once he realized what it would have cost the village.

I still say it is a shabby man who does not avenge his girlfriend's rape, but it is a wise man who bides his time.

I yawned, swallowing some of the dust that danced in the flickering sunlight. The cough that resulted made me sit up with my back against the plank wall.

And maybe, I thought, it is a great man who can refrain from acting on his thirst for revenge and leave the matter to the law.

I smiled as it occurred to me that that was just what the king had promised us back in Oxford. That the law would prevail and England would be governed by its rules.

And now Arnulf and Sigurd had seen what that law was worth. Its weight was determined by the men who enforced it. Arnulf had been forced to kiss the silver good-bye that should have been his to compensate for the wrong he had suffered. And Sigurd? He had seen his chances of revenge evaporate, as well as any hope of getting the woman he hoped to marry. Had he sought revenge and stabbed Darwyn, that piglet of a nobleman, to death when he got the chance? And then wiped Arnulf out for reneging on all his agreements? I had seen young men behave worse than this when they were in love.

I heard rustling from the slaves' bench, followed by a loud yawn from the bed where the mistress of the house lay alone.

I shook my head. It was likely that Sigurd had committed both murders, but regardless my task now was to take him back to Thetford where Winston could weigh in on the matter. And Alfilda, I thought grudgingly.

I heard steel strike steel, followed by a faint whistling. When I glanced at the cooking stones, I saw the flames flare up. The girls were already at work, and I heard footsteps cross the floor as Gertrude joined them. She gave a couple of quiet orders, which the servants listened to, nodding, and then she turned to a couple of waiting farmhands.

I watched in surprise as the men accepted their orders from their mistress, apparently with the utmost respect. Her words were accompanied by small curtsies and hand gestures. The men listened attentively, asked a couple of questions, and then walked toward the door while Gertrude glanced first at the misplaced ladder and then at me. I greeted her with a blink of my eyes. She stood the ladder back up and climbed up to the alcove.

I got up from my bench, slung my sword belt over my shoulder and my shirt over my arm, and headed toward the door.

The spring morning was chilly. Starlings sang along with a few other birds I couldn't name. The sun was up and the countryside was bathed in sunlight, but it was a cold sun, which wouldn't truly warm up until later in the day.

I strolled down to the village paddock, greeted my gelding with a pat on the neck, and then washed myself in ice-cold water from the horse trough.

Since I hadn't thought to bring a towel out, I was shivering and hopping around, beating my arms with my hands in my attempts to get the water on my goose-bumped skin to dry, when I noticed the farmhands busy saddling up two horses.

I said good morning and pulled my shirt over my head, strapped on my belt, and walked over to them.

"Are you riding somewhere?"

They glared at me morosely. One farmhand was gangly, with his thinning hair pulled into a ponytail. The other was a youngster, who withdrew in fear as I approached.

"We're just following orders."

I smiled in thanks for the information.

The gangly one handed the reins to the young one and told him to walk the horses around to warm them up and then put a blanket on them until the mistress was ready.

"So is Gertrude a good mistress?" I asked.

His response was a suspicious glance.

"It's easy to see that you respect her," I explained and continued, "I saw you listening to your instructions in there."

He turned and walked away. A few paces later he turned back to me and said, "The mistress is skillful."

"And a good mistress, as I asked?"

"Yes."

"What about Arnulf?"

He didn't say anything. I saw the younger one behind him, watching me as he led the horses around the paddock.

I walked over to the gangly fellow and put my hand on his arm confidingly. He let it sit there, but I felt his muscles tense under my fingers.

"And Sigurd?" I asked. "Is he good, too?"

"Sigurd?" He licked his lips. "He's a brave man."

"Whom you're going to have to watch be charged with two murders, right?"

His eyes widened. Hadn't the man heard us the day before? His tongue slid over his lips again, then he nodded.

"So help me, I was thinking about telling my master that I believe Sigurd," I lied. "Could Arnulf have killed Darwyn?" I asked, still holding his arm.

"He was a good-for-nothing lazybones." The man spit onto the grass. "He was obsessed with silver and making a big show of himself. Stacked up coins from loaning people money and things like that."

"So he wasn't rich because of the land?"

"Oh, sure." Another glob of spit. "But he was no farmer."

I peered at him in confusion. Then I understood.

"You mean Gertrude runs the farm."

"And he didn't appreciate her," the guy said, moistening his lips again. He definitely wasn't used to talking about his superiors and certainly not with unknown thanes.

I inhaled a deep breath. Things were starting to make sense now.

"Who did he appreciate then?"

"Him?" This time the spit landed between us. "No one. The only thing that mattered to him was silver."

I leaned forward confidingly again and asked, "And then who appreciated him?"

"Huh," he scoffed.

"His neighbors?"

He shook his head and then said quietly, "No one appreciates a stuck-up cheapskate. Some people depend on him, but no one appreciates him."

"Depend on him?" This was getting interesting now.

But he clammed up. Speaking disparagingly of a dead, despised master was one thing. Spilling secrets about that master's men who were still alive, and who would have been this man's superiors, was another.

I tried to get him to open up several different ways. In vain. Finally I tried another tack.

"And Rowena?" I asked. "Now there's a slave girl who seems to be on her mistress's good side."

But this attempt also led nowhere.

I had to give up when he gave me a quick nod and walked toward the stable. The farm *was* rich if there was still hay and feed left to feed the cattle; in other places, folks long ago had to let their animals out to forage in the winter-gray fields.

My stomach rumbled, so I called to the young guy, who had blanketed the two horses by now, to feed my gelding and Sigurd's horse, then I went back to the hall where I found Sigurd, Rowena, and Gertrude sitting around a pot of porridge.

When I greeted them and took out my spoon, Gertrude looked at me defiantly and announced, "Rowena and I are riding to Thetford with you to bring Arnulf's body home."

I had predicted that, and it suited me just fine.

Sometimes it's easiest to control the stallion if you let the mare run alongside him.

19

n the way to Thetford I mulled over how to sneak Sigurd into town without Turstan finding out he'd disobeyed his order not to leave.

The boy rode along seemingly carefree at the side of his chosen one. There clearly was nothing in the world that mattered more to him than Rowena, and truth be told, she seemed to feel the same way about him.

Gertrude rode along in silence on a calm mare, which did not appear to be much younger than she was. Every once in a while she would glance at the two young lovers and the hint of a smile would cross her lips before her attention returned to riding.

It was just the four of us. Before we left the farm, the men were instructed to get to work and the widow told me that two armed men should be enough to secure her ride.

And it was true, Sigurd carried a spear. Not vigilantly in his hand so that it could be lowered at the least sign of danger, but in a leather strap tied to his back. That freed up both of his hands, one for the reins and one to reach out to the wench by his side at regular intervals. The placement of his spear would cause him to lose valuable seconds before he was ready to fight if an attacker should happen to descend on us.

I wore my sword under my left thigh with its hilt jutting out, so for me it was just a question of allowing my right hand to drop and grab the hilt, and I would be ready to fight.

I let the young lovers lead the way, followed by the widow. The gelding and I brought up the rear with a length of about three horses between Gertrude and myself. Should some scoundrel jump out at us and make for the widow or the two young people, who were blind to the rest of the world, I had room to get my horse up to speed, which would add force to my arm strength when I swung my sword.

If you have several armed men protecting a group, some of them can ride in the front, but if you're alone, it's a mistake to ride in the lead. Then you would have your back to the people you were protecting and—when screaming and wailing told you an attack was under way—you would risk being struck down by a spear in the back before you could even turn your horse around.

I also left some distance between them and myself to make any highwaymen who might be lying in wait think that I was not a part of their group. Armed soldiers sometimes avoid coming to the assistance of unknown travelers, so my involvement in their protection wouldn't seem a given to the highwaymen.

There was hardly any way that some scoundrel would try to attack me. The crooks that live off robbing travelers are careful not to tussle with armed soldiers. They go after the easy victims and avoid anyone who even smells of being able to put up a fight.

Of course I wasn't blind to the possibility that not one but a band of robbers might be waiting for us, so I rode with my eyes and ears open, ready to strike first at the least sign of danger. I might not be the most lethal swordsman in the world, but I have never backed down from combating a pack of dishonest thugs. Experience has taught me they're always cowards, ready to retreat at the least sign that they're facing a skilled swordsman with a backbone.

Yesterday's rain had blown away. Instead our cheeks were warmed by the sun, which hung in the east in the cloudless spring sky. The air warbled with lark song and the hoarse cries of lapwings. If I'd had my druthers, I would have ridden with an inviting wench like Brigit at my side, scanning for a cozy spot beneath a Scotch broom or a hollow in the heather, a place that invited lovemaking hidden from prying eyes.

We met other travelers, who all stepped aside for us since we were on horseback. Only once did we have to move off to the shoulder to let four soldiers go by at a full gallop. They didn't even look at us as their horses kicked up a swirl of dust from the path, which we had cleared for them. They thundered onward, doing the business of some nobleman or other.

We rested in a juniper grove, letting the horses graze while we enjoyed cold meat and bread, which we washed down with refreshing ale from wooden casks. After our short break, we were back in our saddles again, and the afternoon wasn't quite half-over when we spotted the fortification that guarded the Icknield Way entrance into Thetford. Now it was time to decide how I was going to smuggle Sigurd into town.

I contemplated simply calling him over and telling him to turn his face away from the guards without making it obvious that he was trying to hide his identity. Or perhaps I should ride in first and try to distract the guards somehow. But before I could make up my mind, the young couple put their heels into their horses' flanks and were galloping straight for the town gate.

Sigurd told me later that they had made a wager about who could reach the gate first, but when I saw him and Rowena take off, I thought something had spooked their horses. I swore aloud, fully expecting to see them thrown off only to be helped up by the guards, who would first brush the dust off their bruised bodies and then ask them their names and what their business in town was—a question I feared the boy would answer honestly.

But then everything unfolded quite differently.

The guards, who noticed the crazed race, stepped in front of the gate to urge the riders on, and then stepped aside to make way for them as they stormed, side by side, through the open gateway. The guards clapped enthusiastically after them.

The leader of the guard, a one-eyed man with a barrel chest, confided in me with a grin that unlike his buddies, he was betting on the wench and thus won himself a tankard of ale from each of the other guards.

I gave him my name and explained that I had brought the widow of the farmer who had been murdered in town, along with her slave girl and spearman. I added that we would definitely be teasing the boy for letting a girl beat him. The guards all laughed at that.

Once we'd brought the horses to the paddock, I led my companions to the inn, where I managed to convince the scrawny Willibrord to let the two women share a room so small that it hardly even deserved to be called a cupboard. I negotiated a price that seemed reasonable given how many people were crowded into town at the moment.

I instructed Sigurd to remain in the room we shared until I managed to track down Winston. When I asked, Willibrord said he hadn't seen Winston since that morning.

He was probably off following whatever leads he could find at the marketplace and in town. I was heading out to go search for him when the door opened in my face and Alfilda's red hair gleamed in the sunlight shining in from outside.

"You're alone," I observed as the door shut behind her.

She nodded and gestured toward a table at the back of the room.

"Did you learn anything?" I asked, accepting the tumbler Willibrord handed me.

"That Harold and Erwin are groveling in their admiration for Winston's abilities."

There was a hint of something I'd never heard before in her voice. She gave me a look I couldn't interpret.

"He's been at the mint ever since you left," she added.

"He hasn't been investigating?" I asked, my brow furrowed.

"Not the murders," Alfilda said, exhaling in a snort. When I gave her a questioning look, she explained, "We do also have that assignment for the king."

I didn't recall her being mentioned in Cnut's instructions, but I let that go.

"But there is some sense in his attentions," she added, reaching up and brushing a lock of hair from her face. "Master Erwin is the king's trusted coin maker, and he knows a lot about what's going on in East Anglia."

I nodded. Winston was the one who'd pointed out that we would be tripping over the reeve's legs anywhere we went here in Thetford. Still, I would have expected Winston to at least *start* investigating the murders as he'd promised Delwyn we would.

"And you?" I asked.

Alfilda raised her eyebrows questioningly.

"Why aren't you with him at Master Erwin's?"

She shrugged. "They're spending half their time singing the praises of Winston's abilities and accomplishments. I'm already quite familiar with those, so I've been at the marketplace most of the time since you left."

It wasn't like her to spend her time shopping, which I pointed out.

She chuckled softly.

"I've been trying to avoid getting tripped up. Which it turned out has been easy since Reeve Turstan apparently didn't bother to warn anyone to set up obstacles for *me*. Although he may have given orders about you two, or at least that's what Winston suspects."

Ah, so *she'd* been investigating the murders. "And have you learned anything?"

"Yes," she teased.

"Let's hear it," I said, leaning back on the bench.

She eyed me for a while and then said, "What about you? Have you learned anything?"

"Why, yes I have," I replied.

"So why don't you let me hear that?" She seemed more encouraging than teasing now.

Nothing doing. I was Winston's man, and she didn't get to hear what I had to say until Winston did. She nodded, understanding perfectly.

"Look, it's the same for me," she said. "I'm Winston's woman, and he should hear what I have to say first. So, if you'll excuse me—I have to attend to something in my room but will be back down shortly." She stood up, gave me an inscrutable look, and headed for the stairs.

I sat there, indignant, feeling mostly like standing up and grabbing her. But I suspected that Winston wouldn't approve, so instead I emptied my tumbler and held it up in the air to catch

Willibrord's attention. As I was doing so, the door opened and
Winston walked in.

20

Winston stopped a couple of steps into the tavern, squinting in the dim light, and then continued toward the stairs after acknowledging Willibrord. I leaned back on the bench, stretched my legs, and yawned loudly. Then I said, "So you're thinking about becoming a master coin maker?"

"Halfdan!" Winston said, turning to look at me. "I didn't see you there. Is everything alright?"

"If by alright you mean to ask whether I have completed my mission and brought you a suspect, well then, yes, everything is alright."

"A suspect?" he asked, looking around at the half-filled tavern. Most of the patrons were conversing quietly over their ale tumblers. One grumpy-looking merchant picked his nose absentmindedly, and two soldiers slurped stew.

"Interesting. Alfilda should hear this," he said.

I said she'd already gone upstairs, which made him put his foot on the first step.

"Wait, Winston! She said she'd be down in a minute."

He looked at me sharply, tugged on his nose, and then headed for a bench at the back of the room, one half-hidden in a shadow that clung to the wall. I went over and sat down beside him so that I could look out at the room. I glanced around. No one was close enough to overhear us as long as we kept our voices down.

"A suspect?" he said. "Are you sure?"

I shrugged and replied, "Someone who has as good a reason to want Arnulf out of the way as anyone else."

"Hmm," Winston studied me. "And Darwyn?"

"Reason to want him out of the way, too. Truly." I leaned toward him. "You see, I arrived at the farm . . ."

"Let's wait for Alfilda," he said, placing his hand on my arm to stop me.

Alfilda? Well, if that's what he wanted. He *was* my master, so I leaned back against the wall and waited.

Finally she came down to the tavern, stopping to scan the room. Winston stood up and walked over to her right away, but instead of bringing her back into the shadows, where I was waiting, he gestured me over and the three of us went back upstairs, the two of them first, Winston with his hand gently resting on the small of her back.

Up on the top floor, Winston led the way to their room, opened the door, and waited while Alfilda and I entered. The window was open, and a sweet spring scent wafted in the window from the meadow outside.

Alfilda sat down on the wide plank bed, pulled her legs up beneath her skirt, and leaned back against the headboard. Winston lay down, tall as he was, beside her, while I undid my sword belt, laid the weapon on the floor, and sat down at the foot end of the bed so that I could look at them. It was an uncomfortable position. After a bit, my back ached.

"Now should I tell you?" I did nothing to keep the sarcasm out of my voice.

"Yes," Winston said, his voice utterly calm. When I glanced at him, I saw he was staring up at the ceiling.

When I first started to work for him, I tended to make my reports too long—a bad habit he never failed to point out. It's not that I needed to limit my speech to "yes, yes" or "no, no," but he felt that I was more accurate when I spoke concisely and clearly.

It really annoyed me, but after a while I saw the sense in his demand, and as time went on I had learned to report my news so briefly and accurately that he hardly ever needed to ask questions about what I'd told him.

For his part, he used to interrupt me often with questions, which irritated me to no end. Now he had grown used to listening in silence to my words without commenting until I was done.

And so I told them succinctly about my evening in the village. I described how Gertrude had received the news of her husband's death, the strange relationship between Rowena and Gertrude, Sigurd's arrival, and what I'd been told about the young people's and Arnulf's reaction to Sigurd's offer to buy Rowena for his bride both before and after the decision of the Hundred Court. Finally, I recounted what Gertrude's lanky farmhand had told me about Arnulf.

"And," I added, "that fit quite nicely with what I had figured out on my own."

They were both quiet. Alfilda leaned back and scratched her back against the headboard. Winston kept staring straight up at the ceiling.

I stood up, rubbing my back to get rid of the pain from having sat in that uncomfortable position, and then walked over to the window and looked out at the meadow where a young couple was very preoccupied with each other behind a row of juniper shrubs. They obviously didn't realize that they were clearly visible from the high windows, since they were otherwise shielded from prying eyes by the junipers.

I turned away, suddenly reminded that Brigit and I had made tentative plans to meet up. I would track her down later.

"And you?" I asked, looking sharply at Winston. "I'm sorry; I hear you were entertaining the mintmaster. But Alfilda?"

Winston didn't look away from the ceiling, just raised a hand and stroked Alfilda's hip.

She complied with this encouragement and said, "I took a stroll through the market. People have been talking about the murders."

"And?" I urged her along.

"And one opinion prevails among the men: Darwyn was killed because he acted unjustly. Arnulf was killed out of revenge."

"But Delwyn is willing to swear himself free. And Arnulf wasn't alone at any point." I stopped when I saw the mischievous glint in her eyes.

Winston just asked, "And what about the women?"

"Ah, the women. Yes," she was looking downright taunting now. "The women know that the good Darwyn made a habit of taking by force what he could not obtain through flattery or kind words or payment."

"Your lady friend has an easier time getting other women to talk than I do," I told Winston. "But if Darwyn was killed in revenge for a different rape, we're obviously going to be busy."

Winston looked me in the eye and said, "In my experience, women prefer to speak to women. And yes, it will be a larger undertaking to figure out all the men who had reason to hate young

Darwyn for what he had done to their daughters and girlfriends—
even their wives, from what I've heard."

I had an idea. "Has anyone else brought charges against him?"

"No," Winston replied. "A few people brought matters up
with his father, who denied the accusations, but most of them
simply chose to accept that they wouldn't get anywhere by going
up against a powerful thane."

"Well, but . . ." I flung up my arms in frustration. "I guess I'd
like to know how many men we're talking about. Or maybe you
already know that, too?"

Alfilda ignored my snide tone and didn't respond. I raised my
eyebrows at Winston.

"I see that you've have already heard about this and are apparently familiar with the cases in question," I told Winston. "And
yet Alfilda told me you had spent your time being flattered by the
coin makers. Was this wrong?"

Winston chuckled as he propped himself up on his elbow.

"Not entirely wrong," Winston said. "I do appreciate praise
from other craftsmen. But the good coin makers are a source of
information. Men come through their workshop, noblemen, mind
you. Not many farmers have call to visit a coin maker, of course,
but noblemen play an important role in this case.

"It is widely held that Darwyn had gone too far. Most people
find it reasonable for a lad to dabble with the lasses, and many are
willing to look through their fingers when a young nobleman
takes an occasional girl by force.

"But no one wants to tolerate someone who repeatedly rapes
women. Those women belong to the thanes' own farmers after all,
the very farmers the nobleman is duty-bound to protect."

"A position that Delwyn apparently did not share," I pointed
out.

"Yes," Winston pushed himself upright into a sitting position. "But his power was so great that his companions swallowed their outrage when he turned them down."

"But he was furious at his son that day at the court," I pointed out, shaking my head.

"Because his son perjured himself," Alfilda said, resting her hand on Winston's.

"Not because of the rape," Winston said. "Perjury is a worse crime in his eyes than the rape of a slave wench."

And then another thought struck me.

"So there must have been a lot of support for Arnulf when he brought his case," I said.

Winston nodded. "People rejoiced that a free farmer finally dared to do what the villeins and other bound farmers and cowardly noblemen had refrained from doing. People didn't care for Arnulf's money-hungry motivation, but they supported him wholeheartedly in his case."

"Oh hell." I realized what this meant. "Then I'm going to have to track down every man who has a violated woman back home. When Darwyn was set free, clearly one of the men who had been hoping Darwyn would be found guilty finally had enough. And killed him."

"That doesn't explain Arnulf's murder," Winston said, shaking his head slowly.

"Because . . ." I stopped.

"Exactly." Winston stroked Alfilda's hand. "The two murders *must* be related. And besides, it would be a fool's errand to track down everyone who had been wronged by Darwyn. Some will have discussed the matter with their friends and neighbors, of course, but most of them will have kept their mouths shut."

Hadn't I just thought that? It's a shabby man who does not take revenge for a rape. And men are not in the habit of drawing attention to their own wretchedness.

"Then what are we going to do?" I said, flinging up my hands, at a loss for how to proceed.

"Well, that's obvious," Winston said, standing up. "We're going to go have a nice chat with Sigurd. That's why you brought him back here, isn't it?"

21

ait a minute," said Alfilda, who was still sitting on the bed. I was already at the door, but I turned around to look at her. She had Winston's attention as well.

"Something doesn't add up," she said.

"A few things," I admitted.

"What do you mean?" Winston asked, watching us both.

Alfilda clasped her hands behind her head, causing her breasts to rise within her thin linen blouse. I looked away.

"Sigurd can't be the murderer," she said. "Well, of course he *could* be, and he had good reason to do it, but that doesn't seem right. Because the court found against Arnulf, he refused to keep his promise that Sigurd could pay the standard bride price for Rowena." As Alfilda proceeded, her voice grew increasingly confident. "But who else would be willing to overpay for a raped slave girl?"

"You mean Arnulf couldn't sell her to anyone else?" Winston absentmindedly scratched his crotch. "Did Sigurd realize that?"

I shook my head. Sigurd was so in love, he was blind to what was right in front of him. "But Sigvald must have realized it," I pointed out.

Winston looked at me. "You said earlier that when Sigurd told you about Arnulf's break of promise, you accused him of following the farmer and killing him. Correct?"

Like anyone, I hate to be caught in a mistake, but now I was forced to nod.

"It's true," I admitted. "I didn't ask him what happened. I claimed I knew."

"Hmm," Winston said with a shrug. "No harm done. We can ask him now."

"But what about Darwyn?" I asked, looking at Alfilda. "Sigurd was the closest to wanting him dead."

She chuckled. "Apart from about twenty other people we've chosen to ignore, yes."

Winston sat back down on the bed.

I wanted to speak, but the look on his face told me it would be pointless. He was staring into space, tugging on his nose, lost in thought. Alfilda and I exchanged glances. I leaned against the door and waited while she made herself comfortable on the bed. A while passed, the silence broken only by birdsong from outside. I glanced out the window, but the two young lovers weren't in the meadow anymore.

Finally Winston got up and said, "Let's go."

We went and fetched Sigurd. He had apparently obeyed my orders to remain in our room, and he was sitting on the bed but leapt up as soon as I opened the door.

"Come on," I ordered him gesturing with my head and leading the way down the stairs behind Winston, who scanned the tavern and sat down at a table.

Winston had also asked Alfilda to fetch Gertrude and Rowena. "I think it might be a good idea to have all three of them together," he said.

While we were waiting for them to come downstairs, Winston studied Sigurd, who returned his gaze, unabashed.

"Your father didn't come see you?" Winston asked him.

The boy shook his head. I glanced over at Winston. How would Sigvald have known that his son was back? I'd sent him straight upstairs as soon as we'd arrived and as far as I knew, he had obeyed my orders and remained behind closed doors until now.

When the women joined us, Winston made sure they and Sigurd sat down against the wall, while he sat down across from them with Alfilda at his side and his back to the rest of the room. I grabbed a stool, which I pulled over to the end of the table. Gertrude had let the two young people sit side by side, and now Rowena squeezed Sigurd's hand. The young lout didn't take his eyes off Winston.

Winston shook his head to Willibrord, who was scurrying toward us. He withdrew back behind the counter with a glance at Rowena. Winston leaned forward over the table. "You disobeyed Reeve Turstan's orders."

"I wanted to . . ." Sigurd began.

"Be with your girlfriend, yes." Winston scrutinized him. "Did you kill Arnulf?"

"No," the boy's voice was hoarse, but firm.

"What about Darwyn?"

I saw Rowena's mouth tremble, then her arm jerked as she squeezed her boyfriend's hand hard.

Sigurd's answer was just as firm. "No."

Winston smiled and said, "I believe you."

Sigurd turned to face Rowena, whose lips curled into a triumphant smile while Gertrude nodded. She hadn't expected otherwise.

"I believe you could have avenged your girlfriend." Winston waved at Rowena dismissively when she looked like she was about to say something. "You seem unafraid. It wasn't fear that held your hand back when you heard about the rape, was it?"

The boy shook his head.

"It was your desire not to provoke Rowena's master," Winston stated this as a fact and Sigurd agreed.

"Arnulf wanted to take the case to court," Sigurd said. "He wanted the money for the fine."

"And if you took your revenge?"

"Arnulf would make me pay the fine that he didn't get from the court."

"On top of the bride price?"

"Yes," Sigurd said.

I had doubted Winston, but now I was convinced. The boy couldn't have asked his father for enough money to buy himself a slave wench.

"But the desire for revenge lived in you and when Darwyn swore himself free, that fed it," I said. "Then when Arnulf refused to keep his promise to charge you only the standard bride price, the thirst for revenge overwhelmed you."

"No," Rowena said calmly.

Sigurd's lips tensed and then he said tiredly, "No, I didn't kill either of them. Ask Delwyn."

Delwyn? We looked at each other in surprise. "What do you mean?" I asked.

Sigurd sighed and said, "When I saw Darwyn walk away from the court, having lied his way out of what he'd done to

Rowena, I was furious and thought only about revenge once the court had let us down."

I remembered him standing next to Arnulf, pale and angry, when Arnulf said that all agreements were now voided.

"But how does Delwyn fit into this?" I asked.

"He . . ." Sigurd sighed.

Rowena leaned against him and kissed him on the cheek. "You don't need to be ashamed," she murmured.

Winston, Alfilda, and I exchanged glances.

"Ashamed?" Alfilda asked.

"It's common knowledge how Rowena and I feel about each other," Sigurd said. "And Arnulf never made any attempt to hide the fact that he wanted to make twice as much money off this slave girl—first for the fine and then from the bride price. He even bragged about it whenever he was drunk." Sigurd glared ashamedly at the table. Then he continued, "When Darwyn went free, Delwyn had me summoned and offered to pay the difference between the bride price and the sum Arnulf was demanding."

He blushed in shame at the thought, and I understood. Instead of taking revenge, he had allowed himself to be bought.

"Sigurd chose me over revenge," Rowena said, sounding proud and defiant. She seemed to be able to read what I was thinking.

Before I had a chance to respond, Alfilda leaned forward and calmly asked, "And if you didn't accept his offer?"

Sigurd slumped and said, "He assured me that I would be a dead man before the sun set if Darwyn fell to my sword."

It was anything but an empty threat when a powerful thane said such a thing to a young farm boy.

"And yet after the murder his angry suspicion was directed at Arnulf, not you. Why? He must have thought you chose honor in spite of your fear of his power."

Sigurd shook his head and said, "No, I was with Delwyn when news of his son's death arrived."

That couldn't be right. I thought back to the marketplace, where I'd run into the farmers, who asked me to keep an eye on their drunken companion. Then I remembered that it had been Sigvald, Herward, and Bjarne, the three men who had sworn with Arnulf, that I had run into.

The boy was telling the truth.

22

inston inhaled deeply and gave me an angry look. As if
I could help the fact that the boy had the best alibi anyone could want for his innocence in this case.

"You might have mentioned that to me before," Winston
grumbled at me.

I didn't even try to hide my annoyance.

"You weren't interested," Rowena told me with a glare. "Last
night you claimed that Sigurd killed Arnulf, and then when he
denied it, you just ordered him to come to Thetford with you."

My look of fury didn't intimidate her.

"Sigurd and I talked about the murders last night, and he told
me the whole thing," Rowena explained, not looking any
friendlier.

I cursed to myself. The wench was right. I hadn't pursued the
matter yesterday. I just assumed that Sigurd was the obvious killer
and let it go at that. Now I understood his frank looks at Winston
earlier, as well as his girlfriend's undaunted behavior.

Suddenly I remembered that Winston had specifically sent
me to the village to investigate whether there were any obvious
reasons for the murder back where the whole case had begun. But
after Sigurd showed up, I hadn't pursued that any further.

There was nothing else to do but to give Winston an apologetic look and let him know with a shrug that I'd screwed up and I knew it.

"So we're back to nowhere again," Winston said calmly. He turned to Gertrude and said, "Mistress, do you have any suggestions as to who might have wanted your husband dead?"

She smiled and said, "Arnulf did not have any friends. That's what happens when you value silver above all else."

That was no answer.

I thought it was about time for me to make up for my shortcomings, so I asked, "What about foes?"

She opened her mouth, then closed it again and sat in silence for a long while before answering. "Foes, no. He was not a man who stood up to his superiors. Nor did he take up arms against his equals. There were those who wished he would go to Hel because he had power over them, but enemies, no."

I seized at her opening. "And who wanted him to go to the shadow land?"

I had once heard a clergyman complain that the Christian faith lay over us as just a thin layer, we who not so many years ago had worshipped the old gods, which the king had only recently rejected, and whom my own grandfather had clung to until his death. One of the things that particularly riled this clergyman was how we failed to understand that the sufferings of hell involved fire, which burned hot. We continued to cling to the ancients' belief that the fate of the wretched in the afterlife would be cold and rain.

Gertrude obviously thought that an afterlife in the heat would be preferable to having to wander around in slush and wretched fog in Hel, and there was no reason not to let her believe that I shared her view.

"If only I could list them for you," Gertrude said with a joyless laugh. "Arnulf didn't *sit* on his silver. It worked for him. He was always willing to lend his silver to a neighbor or someone who came with another man's recommendation as surety, as long as they were willing to pay silver on silver when they repaid it. He never avoided a good deal either, and for him that generally meant one where the other guy lost at least as much as he gained from the deal. Does a man like that make enemies? Perhaps. He certainly ensures that no one will lift a finger to help him up if he should fall, even if they don't personally hate him."

"And was there anyone *Arnulf* hated?" Winston held Gertrude's eye.

The widow shook her head and then began, "Not since . . ." She paused and didn't say any more, but Winston wasn't going to let her off that easily.

"Since? Since what?"

"Since the one he hated died. It doesn't mean anything."

"Are you sure?"

"Yes." Gertrude glanced over at Rowena and then Sigurd, and smiled wanly at them both. "There was someone, but the person in question died a long time ago."

I remembered what King Cnut had told me the first time we met: *Don't waste your hatred on a dead man.*

"In other words, not someone who killed Arnulf for hating them?" Winston said. Like me, Winston knew that other people's hatred can be just as hard to bear as your own.

"No." Gertrude's answer was firm and decisive.

Alfilda, who had been unusually quiet for a while, shuddered and then asked, "Could someone have killed him expecting to inherit something from him?"

"I'm his heir," Gertrude said, suddenly terse.

"The only one?" Alfilda gave me a look I couldn't interpret.

"We never had children," Gertrude said dismissively.

Rowena leaned forward and put a hand on her owner's arm, which brought a brief smile to Gertrude's face.

"Well, if that's everything," Sigurd said, standing up.

Winston glanced at Alfilda and she nodded subtly.

"Just one moment more," Winston said. "I believe Alfilda has a couple more questions."

I looked from Winston to Alfilda. He didn't seem to have any better idea what she was going after than I did, but something important had occurred to her. Her face was placid, but there was a glint in her eye.

"Did you become a slave by being captured by soldiers, Rowena?" Alfilda asked.

Rowena shook her head.

Alfilda turned to Sigurd and said, "You said before that Arnulf made no attempt to hide his desire to earn twice as much on 'this slave girl.' Why?"

"Did I say that?" Sigurd looked slightly stunned from his girlfriend to Gertrude. "That was just . . . Did I say that?"

I thought I saw what Alfilda was going for now, and her next question confirmed that.

"Are you Arnulf's daughter, Rowena?"

The slave girl sighed, but didn't answer.

"I was surprised," Alfilda said softly, as if she were talking to herself, "that Sigvald was willing to acknowledge a slave girl as his daughter-in-law. Not wanting to pay more than the going bride price is one thing, but why not ask his son to give up on the girl and find a free farm girl who would bring a farm or at least an inheritance to the marriage? And now I see why: Sigvald thought that someday Arnulf would be forced to recognize Rowena as his daughter.

"Halfdan, who is a keen observer, told Winston and me that there was something he couldn't figure out between you two"— she gestured toward Gertrude and Rowena—"and I was also surprised you would bring a slave and not a household servant with you when you rode to town to bring home your husband's body, Gertrude."

The widow bit her lip.

Winston, who had sat very quietly, nodded approvingly at Alfilda and leaned forward.

"The truth, Gertrude, please," said Winston.

Her lips trembled, and then she straightened up.

"I was given to Arnulf by my father, who owed him money. He lay with me when the need came over him, but otherwise he preferred the company of a slave woman he had bought for her beauty. In the beginning she refused to spread her legs for him, but whippings, hunger, and imprisonment have broken stronger women. So she lay with him, but never left him in any doubt of her hatred for him.

"When she became with child, he wanted to grant her her freedom and drive me out, but she spit in his face at the suggestion and swore that if he forced her to accept her freedom from his hand, she would kill herself and the unborn child.

"All he could do was say that he would take her son from her as soon as he was born, give him freedom and publicly recognize him as his child; but from that day on, his hatred for her was as ardent as hers for him." Gertrude paused, biting her lip.

"But the baby was a girl," Winston said gently.

Gertrude said, "Yes. And the woman died in childbed."

"And you?" Alfilda asked, leaning forward.

"I had lost a baby a week earlier, a son, who tore my womb apart so I could never become heavy with child again. Arnulf forced me to nurse the girl, because, as he put it, she was worth money. But when he realized I was beginning to love her, he ripped her from me and brought her to the slave house because the hatred her mother bore for him still burned in him. He swore Rowena would pay for the loss her mother had inflicted on him by dying—her death, above all, meant the loss of her monetary value. So yes, Alfilda, it was a slip of the tongue on Sigurd's part, but Arnulf did want to make as much money off this slave girl as he could.

"And that's why—and also because of her mother's hatred—he refused to avenge her rape. That's why he tried to collect the fine and as high a bride price as he could. And yes, Alfilda, Sigvald was willing to do a lot to secure his son's marriage to Rowena."

"But surely Arnulf would hardly let Rowena inherit?" I said, shaking my head in disbelief.

"Hardly?" Gertrude laughed bitterly. "Never is more like it! But if I should outlive him, Rowena and Sigurd knew that I would acknowledge Rowena as my child right away. I breastfed her and let her come to me as often as possible. She *is* mine. She drank the milk that should have nourished my son. She was in my arms the minute Arnulf left the farm. That's how it has always been."

Gertrude paused, watching us with her eyes aglow, and then said, "So call it *my* revenge at that unfeeling layabout of a man, that I should raise up the very person he had pushed down."

Winston turned to Sigurd. "And you told your father about Gertrude's intention?" he asked.

"My father wanted to force me to give up Rowena," Sigurd said. "And marry the daughter of a free farmer instead. What was I supposed to do?"

So we had learned two things: Arnulf was, if it was possible, an even shabbier man than we had previously believed; and Sigvald did have a reason to kill him.

The Trails Diverge

23

o you think Sigvald did it?" I asked.

We were alone, the three of us, after sending Gertrude and the two young lovers away. We leaned over the table and kept our voices down, although that was hardly necessary because of the racket from the patrons crowding the tavern's tables.

Winston didn't respond to my question. He just reached out and took Alfilda's hand.

She let him stroke the back of her hand with his thumb, then licked her lips and looked up at me.

"He has a motive," Alfilda said.

I didn't believe it and said, "But Sigvald could just wait until Arnulf died an inglorious 'straw death' of old age or sickness, then the farm would have gone to Gertrude. Is Sigvald a poor man?"

They shook their heads.

"So Sigurd's inheritance from his father isn't small," I said, my head spinning now. "I certainly appreciate that the more you have, the more you want, but I don't believe that Sigvald would murder Arnulf to get his son an early inheritance."

They didn't say anything. Winston's thumb slid persistently over Alfilda's hand.

"It *has* to be one of the farmers," Winston finally said, breaking his silence.

"Nonsense." I leaned back, staring up at the ceiling for a moment. "Everyone in the village had dozens of opportunities to kill Arnulf. They saw him in the pastures and in the fields, in the woods and behind the dunghill. And he was often alone. Not to mention how easy it would have been to lure him away from the farm to meet somewhere. All an attacker needed to do was entice him with a coin or two. It makes no sense to kill him in the middle of Thetford. Think of the risks! There are people all over the place. The murderer was remarkably lucky that no one witnessed the crime. You can't plan on that kind of luck."

"What do you think happened?" Alfilda asked, pulling her hand free from Winston's.

"Darwyn was the target," I said with a smile. "I don't know what Arnulf saw or heard that made him a threat to the murderer, but somehow he knew something. Obviously it was common knowledge that Darwyn had a number of rapes on his conscience. The law spoke and found in favor of the rapist thanks to the perjury. Maybe Arnulf just figured out which boyfriend, brother, husband, or father had enough courage and a manly enough heart to take matters into his own hands after the court let everyone down."

Alfilda nodded but then seemed to change her mind, shaking her auburn locks. "No," she said.

"No?" I looked at her crossly.

"Arnulf had been doubly wronged," Alfilda said. "By the rape and the outcome of the court case. By killing Darwyn, the murderer avenged that double wrong. So Arnulf didn't have any reason to reveal Darwyn's killer."

"You're forgetting the most important thing we know about that bumpkin," I said, struggling to keep the arrogance out of my voice.

"His love of silver," Winston said.

"Exactly," I said. "Revenge is good; silver is better."

"You mean he was blackmailing the murderer?" Alfilda asked, shaking her head in bewilderment.

"Arnulf refused to kill the rapist even though he caught him with his cock in the slave girl and had witnesses," I said, picking at the tabletop with my fingernail. "Sure, we heard how Arnulf hated Rowena's mother, a hatred that guided his actions toward the girl. But believe me, a man who would rather seek a fine than cool his rage by seeking the revenge that was justified is a man who could turn things to his advantage. And for Arnulf, advantage was the same as silver."

Alfilda nodded reluctantly, while Winston stood up.

"There are two trails—each of you will pursue your own." Winston stretched.

"What about you?" I asked, looking at him in surprise. "Which trail will you follow?"

"I promised my coin smith friends that I would pay them a visit. Which is what I intend to do," Winston said with a nod to me. Then he leaned over and kissed Alfilda's ear and then the back of her head. With that, he left.

My anger followed him across the room. By the time the door fell shut behind him, Alfilda had risen, too. She gave me a devil-may-care look and said, "Who knows, perhaps our two trails will converge."

It was late afternoon by now. The market, which I learned would run for another two days, was at its peak and packed with people and commotion: matrons with serving girls and slave wenches in tow; Vikings on the lookout for nice jewelry or ornate weapons on which they could spend their conquered silver; farmers comparing the prices of woolen items, linen tunics, and shoes with what they'd received for their own goods.

Gruff guards pushed their way through the crowd, while thieves ducked under tent flaps, brazenly darting through the crowd and grabbing a money pouch here, a bundle there, and then rushed off as horrified cries of "Thief, thief!" rang out.

Most of them managed to evade the hands attempting to catch them, but I watched as one pathetic puppy of a robber tripped over an outstretched leg and was brought, struggling and whining, to a large oak tree. There he quickly kicked the last bit of life out of himself, side by side with the swaying corpses of others who had thought they could escape the law of the market, which dictated that thieves who were caught in the act could be noosed up right away, without needing to wait until the hundred's reeve had time to hear their case.

I was still angry at Winston. His apparent belief that he didn't need to inconvenience himself by investigating the murders was one thing, even though he had been the one who told Delwyn that we would clear up both killings if we could. But the fact that he apparently thought he could just leave his share of the work to his woman, that was quite another matter.

I realized one good thing, though, as I squeezed my way toward the wool merchant's stall: my nose was on the right trail, while Alfilda had to go on a wild goose chase that wasn't going to lead her anywhere.

Brigit acted as if she didn't see me when I took up position behind the circle of customers around the stall. Her bony, hard-bargaining husband fawned and sweated, handed over woolen shirts and hats for customers to examine, and obsequiously fluttered his eyelids over his watery eyes as the customers grabbed for shillings from the leather pouches on their belts.

I pushed my way up to the cloth-covered countertop, which rested on two frail trestles. I reached over it and caught Brigit's arm. She glared at me as I pulled her to me, but I didn't care. She could see as well as I could that her tedious, decrepit husband only had eyes for his business.

"Let go of me," she hissed, but she was quiet when I responded by tightening my grasp.

"I'm sorry I couldn't come last night," I said, loosening my grip, although I didn't quite let go. "I promise I'll come tonight."

She twisted herself free and opened her mouth to tell me off—I could tell this much from her eyes—but just then her husband turned to look at us and she dutifully averted her gaze. I picked up a roll of cloth, let it fall again so that it unrolled, and then leaned forward as she reached out to tidy up the cloth.

"Expect me."

She kept her eyes on the cloth, but the quick nod that followed my words was enough for me, and as I left the stall, my anger dissipated.

I roamed through the marketplace until I spotted an ale stand, and took a seat on a long bench across from three farmers. They had obviously had a good day, judging from their rosy cheeks and slurred, drawling voices.

Once my tumbler was half-empty, I realized I had no idea how I was going to set about my task.

If one of the victims' relatives had brought a case to court like Arnulf's, the reeve or his man Stigand could give me a name to work with, but as things stood now I was sure it would be darned near impossible for me to find a single person who had swallowed the shame and injustice.

Farmers stick together like pea straw. I knew that from my time back home on my father's estate. If they divulge secrets to a nobleman, sooner or later doing so will come back to bite them. And in a case like this they were, if anything, even more predisposed to keep their mouths shut.

No man wants a reputation for not having sought revenge when he should have. Unless he's like Arnulf. But there are a lot of reasons why a crime might go unavenged.

If this case had been about a farmer, I probably would have been able to get someone to talk—there's always someone who has a thorn in his side about his neighbor and would be glad to blab his secrets. But Darwyn presumably wronged a bunch of people, which meant that they all had a reason to keep quiet: if one blabbed about his neighbor's shame, he would be revealing his own as well.

I sat and listened to the farmers' drunken talk. Then I stayed for a while after they had left—one of them clearly having trouble walking and needing to be helped away by the other two—and evening fell as I tried in vain to come up with a way to get someone to tell me just one name of one ravished farm wench. I was so preoccupied, I was shocked to look up and notice that the rumble of the market had quieted down and night had settled over the town.

I stood up and slipped quietly down the now-deserted market aisles past the wool merchant's stall, where that whittled-down dotard was lying under one of the countertops on top of a bag of wool. His emaciated chest moved up and down beneath the blanket he had pulled all the way up to the tip of his nose, and I gave him a friendly nod that he didn't respond to since he was already asleep.

Not so, his wife. She was quite awake and complained that I—as she put it—had trespassed against her right in front of her husband.

I was in no mood to be reprimanded. I just asked her if she wanted me to leave, but I could tell from the look in her eyes that that was a dangerous question and that I might not want to hear her answer. So before her tongue got going, I put my lips to hers and my hands on her breasts, and although she protested against my open mouth, I caressed her in silence, and she eventually quieted down. She showed me yet again that she knew how to use her mouth for things other than talking.

24

woke up rested and relaxed. The woman next to me breathed peacefully. She was lying on her back with a little trail of dried spit coming from the corner of her mouth. Her hair was damp. Her breasts, rising and falling, roused me, but as I pulled her to me and inhaled her sweet, titillating scent, she put her hand on my chest and pushed me away.

I was stronger. I grasped her arms and slid my tongue over her nipples, but she slipped free, moved a knee up between my thighs and whispered that if I kept going, she would jab it up into my nuts with enough force that I wouldn't think about sex the rest of the day.

Reluctantly, I got up, found my pants and tunic and put them on, and tightened my belt around my waist. My sword moved easily in its sheath as I pulled it halfway out to test before slipping out the door with a brief, "See you."

I had noticed doors leading into other rooms on my way up the stairs. Now I heard a man clear his throat and say good-bye to a woman I couldn't see, but judging from the voice that responded to him, she couldn't have been much older than Brigit.

I quietly walked down the narrow staircase behind the man, whose footfalls were heavy. I glanced in a half-open door and confirmed what the voice had told me. A girl of about twenty sat upright in the bed. She looked good, with large breasts and raven-black hair cascading down over milk-white shoulders.

There was no response to my admiring gaze. The woman just stretched like a cat in the sunshine, and then crawled back under the covers before I was past the door, which she didn't bother to close.

The front door had shut again behind the man and when I pushed it, I found to my surprise that it was stuck. So I put my shoulder against it, put some weight into it, and when it finally budged, I tumbled out onto the street.

I proceeded into the alleyway, where I tripped over an out-stretched leg, and hit the ground with a groan. I rolled forward and to the left, righting myself. I grasped the hilt of my sword as soon as I was up again and jumped forward, my weapon ready.

An attacker will expect his victim to withdraw in order to figure out how many people he's facing and who they are. Harding had taught me to do the unexpected in situations like this: Hurl myself forward toward my opponent. Take advantage of his sur-prise and thereby gain the upper hand in the situation.

My opponent, however, was no greenhorn. As soon as he tripped me, he followed my movement forward and to the left and now stood ready, with the tip of his sword resting against me.

Then, recognizing each other, we both lowered our weapons.

"You're awfully untrusting. Are you being plagued by dwarves or something?"

Stigand grinned at me.

"Didn't you ever learn that if you tiptoe after a man who's on his way from enjoying another man's woman, he will be sure to strike first?"

He sheathed his sword, and then I sheathed mine.

So I wasn't the only one who understood how to attend to a married woman.

But in this I turned out to be wrong, he informed me on our way to an ale tent, where we agreed to get a bite to eat. The wench I had seen him leave was not married, just betrothed to one of the reeve's spearmen, who, Stigand confided to me with a wry grin, never understood why he was assigned to night-watch duty far more often than his colleagues.

"I don't think he suspects anything, but when I heard footsteps upstairs, it still worried me. I figured I'd better strike first," Stigand said and nodded to a wench with tousled hair that she should set the porridge bowl in front of us. She returned to bring us two tankards of warm ale.

The porridge was rich and full of honey, the malted ale hot and strong, and while the sun burned away the morning fog, turning it into little tufts around the clusters of buildings, we ate our fill and stretched out our legs comfortably at the same time. We raised our tankards into the air and nodded again to the serving wench, who had been watching us without smiling and now grumpily obeyed our demand for more ale.

As we ate and drank, an idea occurred to me. "Has the reeve encountered any obvious suspects?" I asked.

"Suspects?" Stigand's eyebrows crawled well up his forehead.

"Perhaps you don't remember," I chided. "We found a body."

"Oh, that." He said it as if he constantly ran into murdered farmers—which, now that I thought about it, maybe he did.

"My master and I promised to solve the mysteries of the two murders. But maybe you don't remember that either?" I blew on the ale, which was just slightly too hot.

He laughed—deep laughter in that broad chest.

"Yeah, I remember. So does the reeve."

He scrutinized me and I commented, "You seem to be enjoying yourself."

"A manuscript illuminator and his man ride through England, thinking they can hide that they are the king's hounds. Isn't that what people called you in Oxford?"

I nodded, half-annoyed. Only half, because neither of us had really believed we could hide our identities. There aren't that many illuminators in the country, and Reeve Turstan was an important man. He was both rich and powerful, and had surely been present at the meeting in Oxford when we had revealed a murderer and thereby freed Cnut from the charge of having had the victim assassinated.

"And if we are?" I asked.

"Not *if*," he said, grinning openly.

"Well, no," I said with a shrug. "*Since* we are."

"Turstan doesn't think there's any reason for his men to spend time clearing up the murders if the king's own hounds are at his disposal."

This, of course, was flattering news.

"But he promised . . ." I began.

Stigand stopped me with a shake of his head, and said, "He didn't promise."

Which was true, I realized when I thought it over. Of course Turstan was worried that men were being stabbed to death in his town, but it was only truly a concern if murders kept happening and the marketplace was deemed unsafe.

On the other hand, revealing the murderer was not his problem, so he was free to leave that work to us. Once we had the man, Delwyn would be able to avenge himself and then men would hear that peace had been reestablished in Turstan's territory.

I hid a grin at the thought that Winston hadn't realized this any more than I had. He had thought we would stumble over Turstan's men if we followed the tracks left by Darwyn's murderer. Winston often thought more cleverly and effectively than other men, but in this case not so much.

I leaned back and held up my hands to gesture that I'd gotten the message and would drop the subject.

"Tell me about Delwyn," I said, succeeding in surprising Stigand. His eyes narrowed and took on a sharp look. Then he shrugged.

"There's not much point in that. I can tell you the same things as everyone else."

He raised his tankard and drank, snorted over the warm ale, and then wiped his mouth and beard.

"Delwyn owns land all over the place in East Anglia," he said.

I recalled Arnulf telling us that, so I nodded. "A powerful thane."

Stigand gave me an odd look and said, "Uncommonly rich, and powerful enough that very few go up against him. But he's fair."

"So fair that he let his son perjure himself," I scoffed.

"Nonsense." Stigand shook his head haughtily. "Darwyn was a big womanizer, but unlike you or me, who only lie with other men's women when they very willingly spread their legs for us, he liked them to resist. Rape was his game and he took amusement in deriding the men who didn't dare stand up to him. Delwyn certainly didn't look kindly on his son's proclivities, but as long as no one objected, the father couldn't do anything."

"Couldn't? Wouldn't is more like it," I said with a snort.

"Yeah, yeah," said Stigand, waving dismissively with his hand. "Noblemen take what they want, and Delwyn certainly has a bit of that. I called him fair, and you weren't so sure. But you see that when this farmer finally got up the courage and brought the man's son to court, the father forced the boy to show up. For his part, Darwyn had been toying with the idea of paying a call on Arnulf with a sword and a torch, but Delwyn forbade him."

"So he wanted the boy to pay for what he'd done." How odd that Delwyn should consider Arnulf to be a brave man, who gave the nobleman an excuse to teach his son a lesson.

"Delwyn told Turstan that the fine should be collected from the estate his son had inherited from his mother," Stigand said.

"And yet he allowed his son to go free by perjuring himself."

"He did? You know what they said to each other after the court case?" Stigand asked.

I shook my head and said, "No, do you?"

"No. The two of them went off to speak in private, but I know what happened to Bardolf."

"Bardolf?"

"The other lad who swore with Darwyn."

I remembered him. "What happened?"

"Bardolf was here because he was Delwyn's hostage in a conflict with a thane from north of the River Humber. Delwyn had the boy's right hand chopped off for his perjury at the Hundred Court and then he sent the hand to the boy's relatives with a messenger to say that whatever they wanted in order to resolve their dispute, he would pay it."

I gasped. Stigand looked up in surprise, but I made light of it. I didn't have time to explain to him that the last time Winston and I had solved a murder, back in Brixworth, the victim had been a perjurer whose right hand had been chopped off.

"So he let the friend pay for his son's crime."

"*And* no one knows what Delwyn told his son," Stigand concluded, leaning back.

I remembered what Sigurd had said about Delwyn wanting to pay the difference in Arnulf's especially high bride price. Maybe he really was a fair man.

Maybe so fair that he was willing for his son to be murdered to wash away the shame the boy's perjury had brought on the family?

25

After Stigand and I parted, I headed to the tavern, where I found Winston and Alfilda. Winston somewhat acidulously informed me that he expected me to show up at the beginning of the day. I reminded him crossly that the day before he had instructed Alfilda and me to each follow our own trail while he went to sit on his flat ass, ogling at coins being struck.

"And?" Winston said. I was too angry to sit with them.

"And so I'm following the trail I want to follow," I told him.

"Maybe so." He slurped up a glob of honey. "But you work for me, and I expect you to be here when I need you."

I glared at him resentfully and grumbled, "Need me?"

"Need you, yes. You have to go back to the village."

My throat tightened with indignation, and my voice failed me. I turned my back to him and took a few deep breaths before turning around again so that I could see them both.

"To the village? My trail does not lead to the village," I protested. I filled them in on all that I'd learned that morning about Darwyn's argument with his father and about Bardolf's punishment.

"Nevertheless," Winston said, "you have to go back to the village."

He looked at Alfilda, and then she began. "I tried to talk to the farmers we were with yesterday."

I was still so angry that at first I missed the import of her words. Then it dawned on me.

"Tried?" I repeated.

Alfilda nodded. "None of them had much desire to talk to me," she said.

"For any particular reason?" I asked.

A fleeting smile crossed her lips. "At first I thought they were afraid of being revealed as the murderer." Her smile goaded me. I accepted her challenge.

"But unless they were all in on the crime, that doesn't make any sense," I pointed out.

"My thinking as well," she said. "So there must be some other reason that they don't want to talk to me."

And that reason was obvious. I'm sure she noticed the glint of schadenfreude in my eye. So much for her desire to follow the farmers' trail.

I had no doubt that every single one of those farmers trusted their womenfolk to make decisions about running their households. They probably involved their women back home in any decisions they made about running their farms as well. But it was a big jump from that to speaking freely with an unknown woman about murder and legal matters.

"You should have directed them to Winston or me," I said.

"Or some other man, yes," Alfilda said, her smile now gone. "That would have been one way to handle it. I chose another."

I gave her a questioning look.

"I went to see Gertrude and Rowena." She paused, waiting. I looked over at Winston, who had pushed his porridge bowl away.

"And you got something out of that?"

"I'd say so. You remember what Gertrude said when you asked who wanted Arnulf dead?"

"That there were lots of people."

"Not exactly." Her eyes seemed to tease me, and I thought about it for a long time.

"She said, *If only I could list them for you.* So there were a lot of them."

"Maybe. What I got out of her yesterday was that she *can't* list them."

"Because?" Then I understood. "Because she doesn't know who they are."

"Exactly. Arnulf was as stingy with information as he was with money. And apparently not just with his wife. Gertrude and Rowena agree that he didn't confide in anyone. Man or woman," she added smugly.

"But," I said, turning to Winston, "I think we should look at Delwyn."

"Nonsense!" Winston set down his spoon, shaking his head haughtily. "A man doesn't have his own son killed and then ask us to find the murderer."

I looked over at Alfilda, who merely went back to dipping her horn spoon into the bowl in front of her again. She looked as though she wanted to say more, but instead devoted herself to eating her porridge, which must have been cold by now.

"He could be sly enough," I protested.

"For that kind of double dealing?" Winston shook his head dismissively. "He's cunning and powerful for sure, but he didn't murder his own son for perjury."

"So he settled for maiming his son's best friend who happened to be in his custody as a hostage?"

"A hostage in what dispute?" Winston asked.

I shrugged, because I had no idea. Either Stigand hadn't known that or didn't feel that I should know.

"But with someone who was his subordinate without a doubt," Winston deduced. "Someone who didn't have the power to avenge the wrong that was done to Bardolf, but would settle for taking Delwyn at his word and demanding an exorbitant fine. Didn't Stigand say that the maimed boy's family could demand whatever they wanted by way of a fine?"

I nodded.

"Delwyn is powerful," Winston continued, "and men like that are used to getting their way. As you said, his son's rapes bothered him, but he was thane enough to believe that it's a nobleman's right to take what he desires and what he can. All the same, his son's behavior was a thorn in his side, because noblemen are sensitive about their reputation and that of their family. So did Stigand say that Delwyn welcomed it when Arnulf brought the case against Darwyn?"

I nodded again.

"And," Winston said, "Delwyn was furious when his son swore his way out of it with the help of a friend's false testimony. We saw that ourselves. He left the court right away."

"Exactly," I said. "So angry that he killed his son after maiming the friend."

"No, no." Winston shook his head arrogantly. "He's not like that. Believe me, by allowing himself to be talked into perjury Bardolf paid the price for both of them. Only after he was maimed did Delwyn quiet down. You could maybe even say he was disfigured so that Darwyn didn't have to be."

Alfilda pushed her porridge bowl away and glanced up at me. I bit my lip. Winston might be right, I admitted silently to myself. I had met thanes like that back when I was a young nobleman, men who flared up when anyone opposed them, but calmed down again just as quickly.

Wasn't it common knowledge that the king was like that? He ordered men maimed and disfigured when his indignation at having been defied raged in him, but as soon as the blood was shed, he calmed down again.

"So forget Delwyn and ride to the village," Winston ordered.

I wouldn't if I had any say. Hadn't he told me yesterday to follow my own trail? Now he was suddenly going to force me to follow one I didn't believe in just because Alfilda had had a door slammed in her face?

Of course I was too wise to say all that, just as I kept to myself the fact that my reluctance to leave had as much to do with Brigit as my lack of desire to be forced to do Alfilda's work.

"And just what do you suppose I should do in the village?" I asked. I imagine he heard the reluctance in my voice, because there was a chilling look in his eyes.

"We've established that Gertrude didn't know the names of the men who owed Arnulf silver. But certainly all the village men didn't ride to the Hundred Court, and some of the ones who remained behind may know. Someone has to go and question them, and that task is yours."

I gloated to myself in silence at how easy he made it for me before I quipped, "Not only should they be questioned about who owed Arnulf money, but apparently they also should be checked for the length of their arms."

Both Winston and Alfilda stared at me blankly.

"There's no way someone in the village could have stabbed Darwyn and then Arnulf to death. The murderer has to be here in Thetford, and we're going to find him by revealing who had reason to want Darwyn dead—because there are obviously as many people in that category as there are stars in the sky—and who had the opportunity to stab him."

"You're very persistent," Winston all but growled.

"Like your lady friend there, yes. We each have our opinions, and yesterday you told us we could act on them." I purposefully kept my voice quite calm.

"That was yesterday. Today you come in here spewing some rubbish about the murderer supposedly being the boy's own father. That changes everything."

This wasn't like Winston. Usually he never broke his word. I peered coolly into his eyes, and, to my satisfaction, he was the first to look down. When I looked over at Alfilda, she looked back at me hesitantly.

They sure were easy to read. Winston was furious at himself because he had chosen to follow Alfilda instead of me; she was resigned because she'd run into the wall the farmers built between themselves and unknown women.

I waited. Was he going to force me to ride away? That would delay me not only from pursuing the correct trail but also from seeing Brigit. So I cleared my throat and said, "Maybe Alfilda is right."

The astonishment in both their eyes was worth the lie.

"Maybe the answer does lie with a debt-ridden farmer." I paused before continuing. "But if that's the case, he's going to be here in Thetford. Perhaps I was wrong and for at least one of the men in question, his reluctance to talk is because he is afraid he'll reveal too much," I said.

Winston and Alfilda both nodded.

"And if that's the case it would be futile to send me away." I'd set the trap. Now I just had to wait and see if Winston walked into it.

He tugged on his nose. For a long time.

"So you think," he finally said, "that the answer lies with one of the farmers we came here with?"

I kept my voice calm and quiet. "No, but if Alfilda is right, it must be one of them. I still think we should begin with Darwyn."

My master looked at Alfilda. Then he said to me, "You'll stay here. And once you've spoken with the farmers and reported back to me, you're free to follow your own impulses."

Blast it! He'd walked into the trap, but not the one I'd laid for him. I had hoped he would do the talking with Bjarne, Sigvald, Herward, and Alwyn.

26

 hadn't seen any of the farmers since I had returned to Thetford from the village, and although I was furious at Winston and Alfilda, I forced myself to ask them if they had any idea where the four men might be.

"They come and go but mostly stay away from the tavern here," Alfilda said with a shrug. "I suppose they're disinclined to spend money on ale that they could drink for free at home. Our good host does not look kindly on men who take up space at his tables without putting their shillings on it."

So they were in town. Turstan had given them permission to go as far as the town's gate.

I got up, hitched up my sword belt, and started to leave. When Winston's voice stopped me, I turned around grumpily.

"You can forget one of them," he said.

I was about to reject his help, but then realized that the fewer farmers I had to talk to, the better. I opened my mouth to ask him what he meant. Which is when I realized it on my own.

"Bjarne was here in the tavern when Arnulf was killed. Yes, thanks, I can think for myself."

Winston merely shrugged, but I was already heading for the door.

It was cooler than it had been for a long time, which can happen in the spring as the sun and the wind struggle for supremacy. Clouds raced by above the town and the marketplace, and although they weren't ominously dark, there was rain in them. But I'd be damned if I was going to return to the inn for my cape. I pulled my gambeson closed at the neck and headed through the market.

I strolled along, scanning here and there, peering into ale tents and stands. I stopped at the edge of a large square where a group of jongleurs was entertaining an enthusiastic audience and carefully scanned the crowd for a familiar face. I figured the men I was looking for would be inclined to seek out diversions they could enjoy without needing to pay.

Although I took my time and scanned the crowd three times, I didn't recognize any of the clapping, smiling onlookers, so I moved on. I reached the wool merchant's stall and tried to catch Brigit's eye.

As soon as her husband was busy helping a matron with an ample backside, who was touching the displayed rolls of cloth with the look of a connoisseur, I walked all the way up to the cloth-covered counter and leaned toward Brigit, who seemed at first not to have noticed me. But I noticed a blush creeping over her throat, and her chastely down-turned eyes were betrayed by her tongue, which moistened her inviting lips.

I glanced over at the bony old man. He had his back to us, and he was busy extolling the heavy fabrics the madam had just stroked. I reached out my hand, but before I could place it on Brigit's arm, she moved away and once again stood virtuously with her hands folded over her stomach.

Peering at the wool merchant, I decided that he was far too preoccupied to notice anyone besides the customer, who needed some convincing, so I breathed over the stacks of cloth that Brigit should come closer.

She didn't move, so I raised my voice, which caused her to give me an angry look. She mouthed "not here," and then once again stood, the very image of virtue.

I blew her a kiss, turned around, and strolled away calmly without looking back.

Considering the market had been running for five days already, it was astonishing that the stalls and lanes were still so crowded. The thriving market emphasized Thetford's importance as a town. Apart from London, Oxford, and Winchester, I'd never heard of a market that ran for a whole week.

The many languages I heard spoken around me also made it clear the town was bringing in business. There was Danish as it was spoken in the countryside north of the River Humber, as well as the slightly more guttural dialect used back in the old country, and which could be heard all over the place since that was what the Vikings spoke. There were a lot of Vikings at the market. Cnut had paid them in silver and now they were looking for a good deal. The local residents had paid Cnut's heregeld, an inconceivable number of pounds of silver, and now, ironically, some of that money would be making its way back into local coffers.

The Anglian dialect of Anglo-Saxon was spoken everywhere—we were in the middle of East Anglia after all—but I also heard the Saxon tongue I knew from my childhood, along with the drawling West Saxon dialect the men from Wessex use.

There were also people from Kent, who still spoke the funny Jutlandic language. Their dialect is hard for Angles and Saxons to understand, particularly because the Jutes make a big deal about how different their language is and thus don't make any effort to speak so that the rest of us can understand them.

A small group of sinewy, black-haired men, who had settled down in a little ale stand, spoke an unintelligible, rapid barrage of words that, guessing from their clothes and arms, I took to be Scottish or possibly Welsh.

Basically, it was clear that Thetford's annual market drew men from the entire Anglo-Saxon world as well as adjacent lands.

This crowd of different peoples didn't make my task any easier. I'm not a short man, but I don't tower high above the crowd the way I once saw Winston paint a king of Israel in a book. While I can see over the heads of most women and many men, I still hadn't managed to find any of the three farmers.

Whenever I did spot a man I thought might be one of them, he usually ended up ducking into a passageway between a couple of tents, and before I managed to push my way through the crowd, he was gone, swallowed by a new crowd.

I ran into Stigand no less than five times. I saw Harold, the mintmaster's journeyman, darting off three times. And once I saw his master pop up, looking very much like someone who valued his own importance.

I was sweating and hunger was gnawing at my belly. I hadn't eaten since the porridge Stigand and I had together, and by my estimate I had probably covered enough ground crisscrossing these market lanes that I might as well have walked to the village. Then I passed a tent with the scent of roasted meat wafting out of it. I walked purposefully over to the entrance and had just spotted an available seat when Alwyn of the Heath suddenly appeared a few paces ahead of me.

I greeted him and he looked irritated.

"Why so grumpy?" I said with an amiable smile.

At first I didn't think he was even going to respond. He probably didn't either. Then politeness took over, or maybe he just realized it made sense to keep on the right side of a man who'd been tasked with solving a murder. He confided with a colorful swear word that he was sick of walking around idle.

"It's not like there isn't plenty of work waiting back home." The farmer scowled. "But the reeve is a thane and he has no idea about the concerns of a common farmer."

I nodded sympathetically.

"But we can still enjoy a nice meal," I suggested.

"You think I can afford to fill my stomach at any of these places?" Alwyn said with a dismissive snort. "Isn't it bad enough that I can't do the work that puts bread on my table, but now I'm also forced to throw money into the pockets of other cooks?"

"Well, yeah, but you've got to eat," I told him.

This time his response was a sigh, after which he confided that that was exactly the problem. He'd only brought about two days of provisions to town since he had been sure they would return home the day of the trial, but he'd been forced to stretch that so now all he had left was a hunk of dry bread.

In my experience, it's hard to get a hungry man to talk—whereas gratitude often loosens the tongue.

"Believe me," I added. "I know everything there is to know about being hungry and wouldn't wish that on anyone else, so allow me to treat you to a meal."

"You don't know me," he said, peering at me suspiciously.

"Not well," I smiled cheerfully. "But, as I said, I know how it feels to be hungry, and I think what the reeve's doing is disgraceful."

I don't know whether it was the prospect of my treating him or that the meal would allow him to save his crust of bread for later, but he let me lead him into the tent, where I found us seats across from each other at a long, narrow table.

An unbelievably fat woman with wobbly jowls brought each of us a slab of rye bread covered with thick slices of pork and a tankard of ale, which was a little sweet for my taste. There was nothing wrong with the food, though, and we both dug in, chewing pork and bread and gulping down the ale. I was soon licking my fingers clean, while the farmer politely held his hand over his mouth and burped his satisfaction at the meal.

I stretched out my legs, yawned, and asked if he was busy.

"Busy?" His eyes bulged with rage. "Didn't you just hear me complaining over my enforced idleness?"

"You're not supposed to meet the other farmers from the village or anything?"

He dismissed that with a wave of his hand.

I held up our empty tankards and when the fat lady brought us two full ones, Alwyn let me pay for those as well.

"Did you manage to collect on your debt? Someone owed you for some sheep?" I smiled warmly across the table.

His tense body shuddered as if he expected that saying yes would put an end to my generosity.

"Because then you will have gotten something out of your journey," I explained.

Alwyn studied me, his brow furrowed. "Yes. The sheep dealer and I had agreed to meet when the Hundred Court was in session, and my debtor is a man of his word."

I nodded, expecting no less of any man Alwyn would do business with. "And you could get your own debt out of the way," I said.

"My own debt?" His expression was stern. "Who told you I had a debt to pay?"

"No one." I calmly held my palms up in innocence. "I just thought . . . Who doesn't have a debt to pay?"

He straightened his stout body and said, "Not me."

"No?" There was a hint of doubt in my voice. "Not even after paying your share of the heregeld to Cnut a couple years ago?"

I knew many farmers had been forced to put up animals or crops as a deposit in order to generate the amount of silver they needed to pay the army tax Cnut had assessed.

He watched me self-consciously now, and if he hadn't been such a burly man, I would have said he was strutting like a rooster.

"You'll find plenty of men who will tell you that Alwyn of the Heath is not the most insignificant of farmers."

"That's what I've heard, too." I beamed with admiration. "And with a farm that offers good grazing in the hills and fertile fields in the valleys."

He eyed me with suspicion.

"How do you know about the conditions on my farm?"

"You told us yourself when we met at Arnulf's farm. You remember, right?"

"Oh." The farmer calmed down. "Well, it's true."

"So you haven't needed to borrow any money?" I wanted to bring him back to what I was interested in, which was also the reason I'd offered him a meal and two tankards of ale.

"I haven't needed to." Again he seemed cocksure.

"So you and Arnulf didn't have any ties that bound you?"

"Me and Arnulf?" His surprise melted into angry distrust. "Is that what this is about?"

I raised my hand to calm him.

"This is about my wanting to treat an honest man to a meal, a man who is in an undeserved pinch. But now we're having a conversation. And remember that it's my job, as instructed by my master, to shed some light on the murders to satisfy Thane

Delwyn. If you find my questions insulting, I ask your forgiveness."

I wondered whether I'd sized him up correctly. Luckily his response showed I had.

"All is forgiven," he said. He was a man who fell for being asked for his forgiveness by another man. This allowed me, who dressed and acted like a nobleman, to show Alwyn I was inferior to him.

"But, no," he continued, as I had hoped he would, "there was never any money between Arnulf and myself." He paused and then continued with a wry grin. "Not that he never offered, but borrowing money from him was the last thing I wanted to do. I bet he would have collected interest."

"That's what I've heard from other people." I gave him a knowing smile. "And I suppose your neighbors were just as wise?"

"Oh you think so?" Alwyn said, giving me a look that was both sly and cruel.

I raised my eyebrows.

"Because if you thought that, you'd be wrong."

27

pparently generosity pays. A slice of rye bread, a little meat, and two tankards of ale were a piddling price for what the farmer seemed willing to tell me about his neighbors.

I suppressed a smile. I had not misjudged the man across from me.

"It's been known to happen." I leaned over the table and, seeing his confused look, continued, "That I've been wrong."

"Oh." Alwyn ran his hand over his beard.

"Not that I care. But my master expects me to do and think the right thing. So, maybe you would be willing to help me out a little?"

The succession of expressions that flickered across his face showed that he was at a loss. Maybe he already regretted what he had let slip?

I decided to help him along.

"My master is infatuated with his woman and doesn't believe *she* can do any wrong. For example, now he's got it in his head that she's correct in her idea that Arnulf was killed by someone who knew him. I completely disagree. What do you think?"

Alwyn's mouth slid open and his eyes took on a distant look, like someone struggling to understand something incomprehensible.

"Someone who knew him? You mean one of us?" Alwyn mumbled.

"Can you believe that?" I shrugged. "But he's the master. I just obey."

He nodded absentmindedly and then said, "But . . ."

My look of encouragement didn't get him to say any more. He sat there in silence, apparently absorbed in his own thoughts. Finally he shook his head.

"That would only make sense if—"

A shadow falling over the table interrupted him, but I was in no mood to let him stop there.

"If what, Alwyn?" I pressed.

A strong hand grabbed my shoulder. Still, I managed to twist myself free and stand up. My sword was unsheathed the moment I was free of the bench, and as I turned all the way around to face the intruder, I squatted into a swordsman's basic starting stance, with my weapon ready to lunge.

"You live dangerously," I growled to the soldier. "Hasn't anyone told you it's foolhardy to grab men you don't know?"

His ring mail was in good condition, the narrow-necked ax that hung from his belt had an embellished haft, and his clothes were expensive though not pretentious. His blue eyes challenged me from beneath his helmet, and his meaty lips blew into his hanging mustache.

"My master would like to speak to you," he said.

"That may well be." I held my sword ready. "Is that supposed to give you the right to lay your hand on me?"

The corner of his mouth twitched.

"I wanted to get your attention."

"You have it. Tell your master he can find me here in a little while. I have a few matters to discuss with this farmer."

He responded by shaking his head and grunting, "Now."

"Not likely." I smiled coldly at him. "My sword is ready; your ax is still fastened to your belt."

His smile was no warmer than mine.

"Behind you," he grunted.

I glanced at Alwyn, who sat very quiet and straight. He looked over my shoulder and then nodded.

With my sword still ready to fight, I slowly turned my head and looked behind me. There were three spearmen, all with their weapons lowered, tips pointed right at me.

When I looked back at the soldier, he had taken two steps away. Those two steps meant that I wouldn't be able to run him through with my sword before I had at least one spear lodged in my back.

"Your master, you said?"

"Thane Delwyn."

I furrowed my brow. I was expecting it to be the reeve. Why would Delwyn send armed men for me?

"He wants to talk to me?"

"You or your master. *Bring me the illuminator or his hired man.* Those were his words."

Hired man? I snorted.

"Then find my master. I'm busy."

"I looked for him first."

Of course he did. Why make do with the hired man?

"But you didn't find him?"

The soldier shook his head, which got me thinking. I had a clear inkling that if he looked in the mintmaster's workshop, he would find Winston. But had I just received the best excuse I could wish for to give up following the trail Winston had pushed me onto?

The soldiers obviously had the upper hand. Even Winston, who didn't know much about arms or armor, would have realized that I couldn't do anything against four well-armed, determined soldiers. And therefore I also couldn't be blamed for disobeying Winston's command.

On the other hand, I was convinced that Alwyn was just about to tell me something important. What was it that made the idea plausible that one of the farmers from the village was the murderer?

I looked at the soldier and said, "Just give me a moment and I'll come with you."

He shook his head and grunted, "Now."

I bit my lip. Alwyn still hadn't moved. "Would you like to head back to the tavern at the inn and wait for me?" I asked him. "You could enjoy a tankard or two at my expense."

He nodded. I stuck my sword back into its sheath.

"Good then." I turned to the soldier. "Take me to the thane who is so eager to speak to me."

Thane Delwyn wasn't staying at the inn. Nor had he set up a tent in the meadow behind the marketplace.

He was staying in a solid-looking, two-story building. I don't know if he owned it or just rented it while the market was under way, but there was no missing the fact that it exuded wealth.

I was received in a hall on the ground floor that ran the length of the building. From a narrow hallway, I was ushered into the long, wide room, in which hung embroidered tapestries. It looked more like a nobleman's hall than a room in a town building. A high seat occupied the center of the far end of the room, and benches lined the walls. Two other chairs were positioned so that whoever sat in them would face the high seat.

A fire burned on the hearth. Four andirons shaped like dogs surrounded the fire. There were candles in sconces along the walls—wax, not tallow—and two torches flamed behind the high seat, which Delwyn occupied.

The thane calmly watched me walk through the room, sizing me up. So I figured I might as well accept the challenge and size him up in return.

He was just as splendidly dressed as when I had seen him the first time at the Hundred Court. He wore crimson wool breeches wound with wide leather ties. His tunic was of white linen with embroidery around the neck. His doublet was a deep blue, and his sword, which was leaning up against his seat, had an ornately embellished hilt and was stuck in a silver-chased sheath.

His eyes were calm beneath his gray-speckled hair, which, like his beard, was neatly combed. Only a slight tremble at the corner of his mouth revealed that this was a man who had just lost a son, even if that very son had wronged him by openly perjuring himself.

There were no other noblemen present. A row of soldiers stood between the candles along the wall, each with a spear in his hand. Three heavily armed soldiers stopped me at the door and demanded my sword. It wasn't until the axman shook his head that they obeyed my loud protests so that I now walked toward the thane as his equal.

"Am I your man, Delwyn?" I stopped in front of him without greeting him.

His eyes widened in surprise and he said, "Not that I know of."

"So why do you think I will allow you to summon me here as if I had pledged an oath of fealty to you?"

His eyes narrowed and he replied, "I asked you to come."

"Asked me?" I avoided looking at the soldier, who had stepped forward next to me. "Are your invitations always delivered at spearpoint?"

"Sven?" The thane's mouth became a narrow crack as soon as the name was spoken.

The soldier next to me shrugged and said, "Your orders were to fetch the illuminator or his hired man."

Delwyn looked down at my sword. I kept my eyes on him until he acknowledged that he understood.

"I wished to speak with you. I apologize if you feel disparaged by the manner in which you were fetched."

Not that I believed him, but I appreciated that he was wise enough to realize that an apology, although not strictly necessary, was nonetheless appropriate. So I returned his courtesy.

"Well, here I am."

"My son has been brought home. What about his murderer?"

"He may go free," I said. I figured I might as well persist in showing that I would not allow myself to be bullied.

"Free?" Delwyn's eyes darkened and his lips pursed in anger.

"When your men came to get me just now I was in the middle of questioning a man who might have been able to put me onto the killer's trail."

Delwyn glared at the soldier beside me in fury. Might as well continue along the same line, I figured.

"Actually, I asked to be allowed to finish the conversation but was declined."

"Sven?" Delwyn's voice was hard as iron.

The soldier scraped the ground with his foot and then sulked, "You said to bring one of them. Without delay."

"You're right." Delwyn flung his hand up in frustration and then turned to me. "I must apologize yet again."

It would be stupid to gloat, but inwardly I congratulated myself at having earned his respect.

"No harm done. And yet, the man is waiting for me."

Delwyn slowly exhaled, then looked around the hall, snapped his fingers, and said, "Sit down."

I sat down in the chair he pointed to.

A slave brought a little table over, set it next to me, and then stepped aside as a woman placed a silver chalice on it. A similar table was brought over to the high seat. Delwyn poured wine into my chalice from a silver ewer.

"Do you honestly believe the murderer might go free?" He asked and then drank to me.

"Not necessarily," I said, shaking my head.

"Do you know his name?"

I shook my head again and wondered how much I should reveal to him about the disagreement between Winston and myself.

As Sven had led me here through the market, I wondered whether whatever Alwyn was going to tell me might make me change my mind. I had decided that it probably wouldn't. Neighbors always irritate each other, and it was probably just such a squabble that Alwyn planned to bring up.

The only logical connection was that Darwyn had been killed and after that Arnulf had paid the price for knowing something he might not even have realized he knew.

I kept quiet. There was no reason to reveal my disagreement with Winston to someone who would interpret it as weakness.

The wine was sweet and tasted of honey. I took a sip, rinsed my mouth with it, and swallowed.

"Your son . . ." I began.

Delwyn gave me a look of encouragement.

"I hear tell that this wasn't the first time he took a woman by force."

Delwyn became guarded and quietly said, "And?"

"And could you give me the names of some of them? Or more accurately of their relations who might have wanted revenge?"

Delwyn shook his head.

"My son . . . my son took what he thought was his right. But when it was not, I made good on it."

I looked at him, noticed his eye twitching and his mouth tightening in anger.

"You paid them off?"

That would fit with his offer to Sigurd. Delwyn nodded.

"All of them? No one refused to accept payment?"

He bit his lip and I understood. It is possible to make men offers they can't reject.

"There must be some you're not aware of?"

Delwyn slowly shook his head from side to side and said, "You didn't know Darwyn."

I was on the verge of agreeing, about to add a silent "And thank God," when the significance of his words dawned on me.

"He boasted about his conquests?"

A nod, then Delwyn turned his face away. I waited, giving him time until he once again looked me in the eye.

"You were mad at your son. About the perjury," I added by way of explanation.

He took a deep breath and then nodded again.

"Do you have any idea why Darwyn wouldn't let you pay Arnulf off?"

"Because . . ." He inhaled and glanced at the soldiers lining the wall. From the corner of my eye, I saw that they were all looking down. "Arnulf brought the case."

"Oh." I closed my mouth on my own surprise. Everyone else had bowed and scraped when they heard they would be remunerated. Arnulf had hoped to get even more, thus digging himself the grave that he tumbled into after the court ruling.

"Your anger . . ." I began.

Delwyn stared at me.

"You took revenge against this Bardolf lad."

The thane's mouth twitched and he snarled, "That youngster. He let my son degrade himself."

I opened my mouth, but shut it again so that you could almost hear it snap closed.

In Delwyn's eyes, I supposed that made sense. If Bardolf hadn't been willing to perjure himself, Darwyn wouldn't have been able to either. It was a father's logic, I realized.

And I noted something else, too: a man who thought like that about his son wouldn't have killed him. He doted on him too much.

28

I thought for a bit, gaining time by sipping my wine and looking around. Delwyn's wealth was obvious. I was visiting a man who didn't hide his power. And now? What would happen to his wealth now that his heir was dead?

"Do you have other sons?" I asked, setting down my chalice.

"Do I . . ." Delwyn's eyes widened. "What . . . ?"

I held up my hand to stop him.

"If you want to get to the bottom of your son's murder, I'm afraid I have to know a little more."

His eyes narrowed.

"Didn't you lead me to believe a few minutes ago that you were in the middle of questioning a man who could lead you to the murderer?"

I held out my chalice. The thane filled it politely without taking his eyes off me. Did he know I was trying to buy time? Again I considered revealing the disagreement between Winston and me, but again I held my tongue.

"A man who *might* be able to lead me to the killer. In my experience you can never know too much in cases like this. So, if . . ." I left my inquiry hanging in the air.

"My daughter Alburga is married to Asmund, Jarl Thorkell's stable master." The thane's pride was obvious, which was understandable. A marriage to one of the jarl's most trusted men made Delwyn a man of importance.

And, I realized with a jolt, a possible participant in the jarl's power plays.

My heart raced as I took a sip of wine and slowly set down the chalice. Was I close to solving the mystery? I smiled at Delwyn, ran my hand over my forehead, and thought like crazy. The killing could have been a warning to Delwyn. But from whom? Or a way of striking at him. Had he had a falling out with Thorkell? Or with one of the jarl's enemies? Was Cnut's mission for us tied to the solution of these murders?

I became aware of how quiet the hall was. Had I given myself away through my silence?

I smiled apologetically and said, "Forgive me. My thoughts got away from me. It was the name Alburga. My father's favorite saint was Saint Alburga of Kent."

My lie lightened the thane's mood, I could see from his face, which had at first hardened at the thought that I was going to compare his daughter to some random servant, but now softened to realize I was thinking about a Saxon princess.

"And I congratulate you on the marriage. That's quite something."

He smiled self-consciously.

"Almost like having the great jarl himself as your son-in-law, isn't it?" I continued, seemingly ruminating.

"Thorkell is jarl of East Anglia. I am a thane within his jarldom."

Did I detect a reluctance to be too closely affiliated with the jarl's name? That's how his response struck me. Not the jarl's thane, but a thane within his territory. Had Delwyn not pledged an oath to Thorkell?

"Were you in Oxford?" I asked.

He stared at me blankly and then said, "I feel like you skipped something there."

"With your leave, allow me to explain. Did you participate in the large meeting in Oxford, where Cnut swore to uphold the laws of England?"

Delwyn nodded. I could see in his face that he was trying to figure out where I was going with this.

"And were you one of the thanes who pledged their oaths to Cnut?"

Yet another nod, reserved this time.

"Get to the point," Delwyn said. "I don't see what this has to do with my son being killed."

How far should I go? How far could I trust this rich and powerful thane? I decided to follow my brother's advice from ages ago: Never trust whores, dogs, or noblemen. So I sidestepped the issue.

"Had your son pledged an oath to anyone?"

Delwyn shook his head. "He didn't have any land yet or a title. Where are you going with all this?"

"Hard to say," I said. "In my experience, murders are often solved by connecting two pieces of information that don't seem related but which become crucial when you figure out how they're connected." One lie more or less wasn't going to matter, so I continued, "One time we solved a murder because a girl said the dead man's dog hadn't barked all night."

The thane looked at me in confusion, so I hurriedly continued. "Unbelievable, right? That a dog's silence could end up solving a murder? But now you see how information that seems random and insignificant can turn out to be enormously important."

I could tell from his eyes that he did not see this at all, but also that he was willing to let me continue.

"What I was thinking is . . ." I realized I was going to have to lift one corner of the blanket I'd thrown over my disagreement with Winston in order to maintain my credibility. "Isn't it most likely that your son was killed by a nobleman?"

Delwyn flung up his hand in anger.

"I paid off all the farmers whose women he'd molested. But he was wise, that boy, and steered clear of noblemen's women. So, no. And I remember your thoughts about Arnulf's death."

I stared at him, uncomprehending.

"That he was stabbed with a knife, so my men and I were cleared of the charge."

Which was true. Darwyn had also been killed by a knife. Was Alfilda right? No, I decided. Everyone carries a knife. A nobleman who's trying to hide his crime might keep his sword in his sheath and attack with his knife.

And the same was true of whoever killed Arnulf.

With some effort I managed to keep my face calm so as not to give anything away. I'd grasped at the right end this time. Both men had been killed by a nobleman, one who knew how to hide his crime.

"Maybe I was wrong about the knife," I said, as calmly as I could.

Delwyn's head whipped up. "Are you accusing me of killing the farmer after all?" he asked.

I shook my head and soothed him, "Then we'd be dealing with two killers, because you certainly didn't kill your own son."

He hissed in irritation.

"Well, I'm sorry," I said, "but that's how it is."

He glared at me and said, "Do you think there are two culprits?"

I looked him in the eye and shook my head.

"So, we're looking for a nobleman." I straightened up to give my words and myself more weight. "Who?"

He thought it over. For a long time. I could see from his face that he believed me.

"No one comes to mind. My son didn't have any enemies."

Aside from an unknown number of farmers, but I didn't say that out loud.

"And you?" I asked.

"Me?"

"Who are your enemies?"

After slowly shaking his head, he said, "No one who would strike like that."

There was no way he could know that. Men try to take revenge in strange ways.

"Someone who didn't dare stand up to you, but wanted to hit you through your son." I took a deep breath and decided to take the plunge. "Someone who is powerful enough to dare to do it."

His eyes emptied of expression and when they took on some liveliness again, he leaned forward and said, "Thorkell?"

My response was silence.

"No." He shook his head. "The jarl has no reason to want me to suffer. I never withhold men or money when it's needed. I come when he orders and remain until he grants his army leave to go home."

Not a word about underhanded dealings. Either he was wiser than I'd thought, or he had no knowledge of any deviousness by the jarl. If the first were the case, I realized, another powerful man might be behind the murders. But I didn't dare mention Cnut's name in this context.

I mulled over a thought that was so audacious I wasn't sure I dared to express it and instead raised my chalice, drank, and then decided if I didn't ask the question, I would regret it later.

"Your son's appetite for women," I began cautiously.

He interrupted me. "Haven't we discussed that enough?"

"What did your wife think about that?"

The thane raised himself halfway up in his seat, then sank back down. "Darwyn's mother died five years ago."

No hint about whether he had taken a new wife, so I was forced to pry.

"It's not easy for a man to live alone."

I saw him clench his fists. He understood where I was going with this. His voice was hoarse when he responded. "Unlike my son, I have never taken a woman against her will, so you can spare yourself your current line of deliberations."

So the son wasn't killed to frighten the father from acting like him.

"Your daughter, then? How did she view Darwyn?"

I'd overstepped the line, or perhaps Delwyn had had enough for other reasons. He stood up so suddenly that the little table next to him tipped over and the ewer and chalice clattered to the floor.

"Bring me my son's murderer," he commanded.

I remained seated, hoping my calmness would convince him to sit down again.

Sven's grip on my shoulder was as hard as before. He pulled me up. I kept my eyes locked on the thane, who stared back, enraged. I relaxed my muscles and jumped when I felt Sven's grasp loosen.

Without a word to Sven or anyone else in the hall I walked toward the door with as much decorum as was possible.

One Trail

29

The clouds had come in while I'd been with the thane, and the first raindrops began to fall as I jostled my way through the crowd. A cold spring rain, no doubt longingly awaited by the farmers, made me pull my gambeson shut at the neck.

Had I learned anything?

I stopped by a pigsty surrounded by a wattle fence. The owner had likely claimed this piece of land from olden times since his pigs were now grunting around in the middle of market stalls, the closest of which belonged to a honey-cake baker. That baker was probably none too happy about his porky neighbors.

Delwyn had summoned me because he was understandably curious how far we'd gotten in determining who had murdered his son. Had I put him at ease? And had I learned anything useful myself?

Delwyn didn't seem to be involved in any underhanded dealings among the nobility. He didn't share his son's proclivities to forcibly lie with women, but behaved dutifully toward the jarl and the king, whose man he was.

Was there anything in that? He hadn't given his word to Thorkell, but that might have been because he mistrusted the man. Or maybe just saw through his power plays and chose to stick with Cnut.

And yet . . . His obvious pride at his daughter's marriage to Jarl Thorkell's trusted man spoke against this.

Was he simply the honest thane he seemed to be? A nobleman who added riches to power by looking after his own affairs and giving each superior what he was entitled to? A father, whose weakness was that he couldn't keep his son in check?

The son . . . whose repeated offenses the father had paid for. Paid quite a price for, as I understood. Delwyn would rather cover the palm of a wronged man with silver than watch that same man walk away thirsting for revenge.

Because he had feared for his son's life, of course.

I kicked at the wattle fence, which caused a fat sow to chew her food angrily at me, exposing her yellow teeth. I ran a finger around my collar to wipe away the raindrops that were tickling my skin.

It wasn't noble-mindedness that made Delwyn pay—overpay— for his son's offenses, but fear that the boy wasn't up to tackling a man who was out for revenge.

And did Delwyn really know about all the men whose women his son had accosted? Wasn't there a man walking around some- where, pleased to have finally exacted his revenge? A man—a nobleman—whose holdings were perhaps not as great as Delwyn's, and yet sizable enough that his duty to seek revenge ranked above his love of silver? A man who had said no to the thane's offer to pay him off?

No, Delwyn would have thought of that himself and the avenger would have felt his retribution. And Delwyn seemed con- fident that he knew all of the men who might conceivably take revenge. Darwyn hadn't kept quiet about the women's thighs he had opened by force. He had bragged about them outright.

Yet there could still be one the boy had failed to disclose.

I strolled along the fence to the honey-cake stall, and handed a square *klippe* coin to the toothless crone, who placed a sweet-smelling cake in my hand. Her awning extended over her stall counter, so I stood under it to get out of the rain while I munched on the cake, my back to the baker and the woman.

Someone who was so powerful that the lad didn't dare boast about having abused his woman. I swallowed a crumb the wrong way and bent over coughing into my hand. This caused me to drop the rest of the honey cake in the dust below, which was slowly turning into mud from the rain.

Someone who was more powerful than Delwyn.

A man like that couldn't be hard to find. There could hardly be more than a handful of noblemen in East Anglia who exceeded Thane Delwyn in riches—maybe five more who exceeded him in power. But all ten wouldn't be in Thetford, so finding the ones who were seemed doable.

Then, a thought struck me.

Delwyn might not have been wrapped up in underhanded dealings, but what if Darwyn was? It's been seen before that a young sapling, whose father obviously shields him from responsibility, pads his life of ease by participating in underhanded dealings, which the young man considers merely a way to pass the time.

He didn't have any land yet or a title, Delwyn had said. A nobleman's son generally received land and responsibility long before he reached the age of twenty, and Darwyn was at least twenty. By the time I was fifteen I was leading a platoon of my father's soldiers, and only my father's desire to ensure himself an heir should Harding fall had caused him to order me to stay home when the two of them rode alongside King Edmund Ironside to their deaths.

I pushed the thought away. I couldn't see why Delwyn had prolonged his son's puppy life, but I was convinced that the lad wasn't maneuvering to gain power: his reputation as a rapist and violator of women would preclude that. What nobleman strategizing to increase his power would have trusted Darwyn?

Our killer had to be a thane, one so powerful that Darwyn hadn't dared to brag about his exploits.

All I had to do now was convince Winston that this was the case and then find out which noblemen of that ilk were staying in Thetford.

With my head bowed to the now pouring rain, I headed toward the tavern so that I could find Winston as quickly as possible and move forward with the case.

People were scurrying away from the market. Those who could fit into the ale tents were crowding in there. Others hurried down the walkways and alleys, and if these had been congested before, people were now openly pushing and shoving to get through and out of the cold raindrops.

I cut across a little square I recognized not far from the tavern, rounded the corner of a market stall, and walked smack into a figure who had stood still so suddenly in front of me that I didn't have a chance to stop.

Cursing, I reached out and grabbed the man's arm to keep him from falling while using him to hold myself up in the slippery mud beneath my feet.

"Relax," I said. The man turned to face me and I found myself staring into Winston's face.

"You're sure in a hurry!" he said.

"It's raining, and I'm wet. Why did you stop?"

"To keep from falling." Winston's outstretched hand drew my attention to a rope that ran from the top of the tent down into the grass that was helping to hold up the stand.

We jogged on, reached the square in front of our inn, and got to the door at the same time. Winston darted inside just ahead of me.

The tavern smelled of wet clothes. The place was packed. Everyone seemed to be taking shelter from the rain. At a table right in front of the counter, I greeted Gertrude, Rowena, Bjarne, and Sigurd, who had just turned to look at the stairs where his father was coming down, chatting with Herward. The two farmers acknowledged us as we stood there dripping and then walked over to sit down at the table with the other villagers.

Alfilda came down the stairs behind the two farmers and went straight over to Winston.

Winston shook himself off, water splattering, and then strode purposefully across the room to a table by the wall, with Alfilda following. I loosened my belt, pulled my gambeson off, and shook some of the rain off it before following Winston. I wrapped my sword belt around my wet gambeson as I walked.

By the time I reached them, Winston had taken a seat with Alfilda next to him. I leaned my sword against the wall and the host came hurrying over to us with two steaming tankards, placing one in front of each of us and asking Alfilda if she also wanted something to warm her up. She politely declined.

We drank and I shivered, but since my shirt was as good as dry, I didn't bother to go up to my room to grab a tunic to put on over it.

"Well?" Winston set down his tankard and gave me a look of encouragement. "Do you bring news?"

"Yes," I said. "I've just come from Delwyn."

"Delwyn?" Winston pursed his lips and scowled at me. "I thought I told you to talk to the farmers." Then he gestured at a table behind me with his head and rather snidely said, "But perhaps you couldn't find them?"

"I found Alwyn and I was talking to him, but I was interrupted and forcibly taken to see Delwyn."

Winston leaned back against the wall and said, "Do tell."

As usual they listened in silence to my report, which I made brief and yet as accurate as possible. I started with the axman grabbing me at the ale stand and ended by recounting the thoughts I'd had by the pigsty and the honey-cake stand.

"Hmm," Winston said and then was quiet for a bit. He turned to Alfilda and said, "So you were wrong?"

Alfilda bit her lip and said, "Halfdan is onto something . . . something correct. His thoughts are clear and sensible. But they are thoughts, not evidence."

I stood up from the bench in irritation, then sat down again, staring across the table at her. "Of course they're thoughts. That's how we work, Winston and me. We have yet to solve a murder case by having the murderer walk up to us and profess his guilt. We talk to people, listen to them, try to catch them contradicting themselves, and then we *think*."

Winston hadn't said anything during my tirade. Now he looked at Alfilda and said, "Halfdan is right. That's how we work: try to find the details of the case and then gather them into a bigger picture." He looked across the table at me. "You've done that well, Halfdan, and your thoughts are sensible and well worked through. But Alfilda is right. It's not evidence. What do you plan to do now?"

I should have thought that was obvious.

"It can't be that hard to identify the handful—at the most—of noblemen who are in Thetford and powerful enough that Darwyn didn't dare tell his father that he'd committed an offense against one of them. After that it's just a matter of tracking them and getting them to talk."

"Good," said Winston, tugging on his nose.

I stood up to begin my pursuit before Alfilda could get Winston thinking about something else, but he stopped me.

"You said you spoke to Alwyn. What about?"

I sat back down and recounted the conversation as carefully as I had just done for the conversation with Delwyn. They listened again in silence.

"So Alwyn was going to wait for you here?" Winston got up halfway from his seat and scanned the room. "He's not here."

I shrugged.

"He probably changed his mind."

Alfilda had listened quietly for a long time, but now she leaned forward and said, "That would only make sense if *what*?"

I stared at her blankly.

"*That would only make sense if . . .* that's what you said Alwyn said."

"Oh, right, but . . ." I'd actually forgotten all about that until I'd recounted my conversation with Alwyn to them.

"Why don't you just find him before you head out? It's still raining anyway." Winston gave a decided nod as if that settled the matter.

I stood up crossly and looked around. Winston was right that there was no sign of Alwyn here in the tavern. I walked over to the farmers' table. They were preoccupied with their conversation but looked up when I reached them and asked if they knew where Alwyn was.

"Alwyn?" They asked in a chorus, as they glanced at each other.

Herward glanced at Sigvald and said, "Didn't Alwyn go out on his own this morning?"

Sigvald nodded and said, "I think so."

"He was sitting here a little while ago," said Bjarne, who pretty much otherwise never opened his mouth. "I suppose he went upstairs."

I smiled at them. It was a bit late for a midday nap, but nap or no, my master had given me an order, and I was eager to complete it so that I could get back to following my trail. So I headed upstairs.

On the second floor I made my way to the farmers' room, knocked, waited, and then knocked again. When there was still no answer, I pushed on the door, which wasn't latched, and stepped into the room, which smelled faintly of ale. Then I cursed loudly, realizing that I had been following the wrong trail.

I stormed back downstairs to the tavern to tell my master—and his woman—that Alwyn lay dead in his bed, a bloody wound in his chest.

30

stopped on the stairs and glared at the farmers, who were still jabbering away at their table. One of them had ruined my investigation, and I was in no mood to let the guilty party get away with it.

Sigvald noticed me staring at them and furrowed his brow at me in puzzlement, but when I just stood there, he went back to his conversation with Gertrude, who had her back to me. Sigurd and Rowena sat across from her, so absorbed in each other that I suspected you could stab a man to death in front of them and they wouldn't notice.

At the end of the table closest to me, Bjarne and Herward were leaning together engrossed in conversation. Herward glanced up briefly at me and then returned his attention to his companion.

One of them did it. Which one?

I thought back. Did Alfilda know something that was hidden from me? Hardly. She'd been guessing, just like me. The only difference was that she'd guessed correctly.

Winston noticed me standing there. He scrutinized me for a moment, then stiffened and stood halfway up. I nodded to him, turned, and walked back up the stairs without waiting for him to follow me.

I stopped in front of the door. Winston and Alfilda caught up, wondering what was going on.

"Would you look at this mess?" I said and pushed open the door.

Alfilda used to run a tavern and she had probably seen her share of beaten-up men, goose eggs, and bloody noses. All the same, I heard her catch her breath, deeply shocked at the sight of the bloody figure on the bed.

"Was that really necessary?" Winston asked glaring at me. I shrugged. I hadn't asked her to come upstairs. If she wanted to be a part of our work, she ought to shoulder her share of the unpleasantries.

"When?" Winston was leaning over the body. "Close the door."

I obeyed.

"It's hard to say." I put a hand on the dead man's forehead. "He's cold, but the blood hasn't congealed yet."

"Hmm." He waved his fingers over the body a hand's width above the chest. "One . . . two . . . five stab wounds. What about Arnulf?"

"He was also stabbed several times." I realized what that meant. I'd overlooked the fact that the killer didn't know how to kill someone quickly and effectively.

Noblemen, like myself, are trained killers. I wasn't even ten before my father and Harding were forcing me around the training grounds. But trying in vain to fend off their blows taught me something more than just how to take a beating.

Both of them showed me the right places to aim when stabbing an enemy's body. They showed me where a sword's blade should hit to slice deep into an artery, where to strike with an ax to crush bones and slice tendons and blood vessels.

This killer did not know any of this. He stabbed at random, his knife sticking into the body multiple times to inflict as much damage as possible until the victim bled to death.

Arnulf had been lying on his stomach, I remembered, with his hand clutching his right side. I looked at the cut in Alwyn's throat, his hole-riddled shirt, and what was likely the final deadly stab up under the breastbone.

I reassured myself that a wild, enraged man could have done this, unable to control himself, just stabbing and stabbing. Even a nobleman could snap like that.

Before that thought had taken root and made me forgive myself for my own lack of insight, I realized how wrong it was.

An out-of-control murderer would attack in a fit of rage, stabbing and jabbing, slicing and tearing.

This killer had not done that. Arnulf's throat was cut, and then he was stabbed through the tunic in multiple places before finally receiving the fatal blow, angled upward into his heart. That was the mark of an incompetent knife wielder, not a nobleman in a fit of uncontrollable rage. A nobleman would have known to stab deep and upward on the first thrust.

Looking at Alwyn's body, I saw the same thing. Five random jabs. One had struck his neck without cutting the artery, an error no man with weapons training would have made. A second thrust caught Alwyn in the shoulder, where it would surely have hurt, but would not have been life-threatening. The third blow had hit the upper right side of Alwyn's abdomen, where I could see it had slashed his liver. The fourth and fifth stabs hit the right side of his chest. The one under his breastbone was deflected by his ribs, and the other went deep into the middle of his abdomen. This stab must have hit an artery, because the blood had gushed out of this wound with as much force as the slashed liver. It was hard to say which had killed him. My guess was that between the two cuts to his liver and abdomen, there had been a fatal loss of blood.

The frustrating part of it from our perspective was that no artery had been cut. Blood had gushed but not splattered. It was possible that the killer could have avoided getting blood on himself.

Aside from his hands, of course. I looked around. There was a shirt on the floor to the left of the bed. I picked it up and showed it in irritation to Winston. The killer had used it to wipe his hands.

Alfilda hadn't said anything since entering the room. I bit my lip, turned away from her, and glanced at Winston, who was still looking at the body. Then I realized there was no getting around it.

"You were right the whole time," I told Alfilda. The words stuck in my throat, but they had to be said. "It was one of his neighbors."

Alfilda gave me a look I couldn't interpret, and then she put her hand on my arm. I didn't try to shake it off.

"I had my doubts," she said, "until I saw this. What do we do?"

Her question was directed at Winston, who didn't seem to hear it. He was standing very still, his eyes half-closed. He tugged on his nose and then gave us both a look to indicate that we should be quiet.

Some time passed. The only sound came from a fly buzzing over the dead man's chest. Every time it settled, Alfilda chased it off with her hand.

"For a long time I believed a nobleman was behind this." Winston announced this so suddenly that both Alfilda and I jumped.

"I don't believe that," I said, staring at him. I didn't need him to try to smooth over my mistake.

"Because I listened to Alfilda?" He gave me a penetrating look.

I nodded.

"You have often let me know what advice your brother gave you," Winston said. "Now let me tell you one my mother told me: A wise hen has many nests."

Winston looked back at the body, and Alfilda chuckled.

He smiled wryly at me and said, "Unlike you, Halfdan, I am aware that I make mistakes."

I was about to respond, but he held up his hand to stop me.

"I finally realized this morning that Alfilda was right," he said.

I didn't even try to tone down the skepticism in my face.

"You've been letting me and Alfilda do all the work while you sit around on your hams with the coin makers," I protested. "How is it that you were able to decide anything this morning?"

Winston chuckled. "Sitting around on my hams? Indeed. I believe I already mentioned to you that the good coin makers are sources of knowledge, but perhaps you didn't hear me?"

I did not care for his mocking tone.

"I believe I also mentioned that a steady stream of men comes through their workshop," he continued. "And I even added that most of them are members of the aristocracy. But you see, Halfdan, when you're dealing with noblemen, it's often a good idea to question other noblemen. Which is just what I've been doing.

"To be sure, I haven't minded the admiration of Erwin Mintmaster or Harold, and I enjoyed being able to help them by offering them a couple of sketches of Cnut they can use if they someday become accomplished at converting drawings into the dies they use to mint the coins.

"But my most important reason for cultivating my friendship with them was so I could—how to put this?—well, yes, sit around on my hams and let the information come to me.

"The local nobility were extremely tired of Darwyn's behavior, as I believe I mentioned before. Was one or more of them so tired that they decided to kill him to put an end to it? That was my idea, and I pursued it."

I raised my eyebrows, wondering if he was pulling my leg, but he appeared to be earnest. And then it occurred to me that I should have thought of that as well. I glanced at Alfilda and was relieved to see that she was as surprised by this as I was. At which point I couldn't help but chuckle.

They wondered why I was chuckling, so I explained, "So, we've each been following our own trail."

They smiled, and I noted that Winston seemed relieved.

"And that's not a bad thing since one of the three trails led in the right direction." Winston gave Alfilda an admiring look. "But believe me, Halfdan, I was just as uncertain as you while I was questioning all the noblemen who came through the workshop. Of course it had to be done tactfully so they didn't suspect what I was really up to, but luckily tact is one of my strong suits, and I'm positive none of them suspected anything.

"And this morning I was sure. None of the noblemen had knowledge of anyone taking matters into their own hands, let alone that Darwyn had even made the mistake of assaulting a nobleman's woman."

I looked up, astonished.

"I thought that if each of the three of us pursued our own trail, one of them would surely turn out to be the right one. Then when it turned out that the farmers wouldn't talk to Alfilda, I had to send you down her trail."

I opened my mouth to speak, but he beat me to it. "After all, I knew that your trail and my own went the same direction."

"You might have mentioned that," I said.

He slowly shook his head, a mischievous twinkle in his eyes.

"We all have different things that motivate us to do our best. For you, it's anger."

He had been provoking me on purpose! I felt a surge of that anger deep down, but then I realized he was right. My indignation at being told to pursue a trail that I believed was wrong instead of the one that I thought was right made me work harder.

"Don't make a habit of it," I said.

"Sometimes the horse should feel the whip, other times the spurs," Winston said, holding his hands up as if to say *what's the big deal*. "As if you never goad me."

He had a point, so I didn't say anything.

"What do we do now?" Alfilda asked.

Winston raised his eyebrows at me and asked, "Sigvald?"

"Or Herward," I replied. "We agree it probably wasn't Bjarne."

"Because he was here when Arnulf was killed?" Alfilda asked, scratching her arm. "But *was* he?" She waited until she had our full attention before continuing. "He was here when Arnulf went out. As far as I can remember, he sat down at a table with some other men. But how long did he stay?"

"I don't know," I said with a shrug. "I went out."

"But we stayed here." Winston closed his eyes halfway. "I believe he was still sitting there when we went to bed."

"I think so, too," Alfilda said. "But are we sure?"

"Are you confident Arnulf was murdered in the evening?" Winston asked, eyeing me sharply.

"As I said, his clothes were damp, but his back was dry. If he'd been killed in the morning, the dew would have wet his back as well."

"I'm quite sure Bjarne was here the whole evening," Winston said and leaned against the wall. "And wouldn't people have wondered what he was doing if he went out late at night?"

"Men have been known to go out late at night," Alfilda said with a faint snort.

"A whore?" Winston said, nodding. "We won't rule him out."

"We should inform them of Alwyn's death, shouldn't we?"

Winston shook his head. "Let's keep that to ourselves for as long as possible." He suddenly looked up. "Sigvald shares this room with Alwyn, right?"

I nodded and then suddenly remembered Arnulf had shared this room also.

"With both of the dead men, Alwyn and Arnulf," I said.

"Hmm. Of course that *could* be significant. But at any rate, like I said, let's keep this information to ourselves for a bit so we're the only ones who know about it."

"It's too late for that," I said.

Winston seemed puzzled, so I pointed out that the murderer also knew.

"Of course," he waved his hand in irritation. "Let's get on with this."

31

We'd just started down the stairs when we heard someone coming up. A quick glance revealed that it was Sigvald. He was huffing and puffing, gripping the railing, and it took him a minute before he noticed us and tipped his head back with difficulty so that he could see us. He was soused on the tavern's good ale, and he was struggling to focus.

I glanced at Winston, who nodded faintly and took a step back. Sigvald shook his head and again began his cumbersome climb toward us. We awaited him in silence.

"Aren't the stairs wide enough?" he asked once he reached us.

Winston smiled politely and said, "Indeed, but we'd like a word with you."

"I need to lie down."

"But before that . . ." Winston began.

Sigvald held his hand up in objection and grumbled, "Shut up. I'm going to bed."

"That will have to wait," Winston said in the sharp voice of a man who wanted to be obeyed. "Halfdan!"

I complied, grabbing hold of Sigvald and guiding him purposefully toward the next flight of stairs that led up to the top floor. He tried to resist, but his skinny body was no match for mine. I basically lifted him up and set him on the first step before loosening my grasp.

"Would you like to walk on your own?" I asked him.

In response he took a swing at me. Not a swing with any strength in it—aside from not having much of a build, he was also drunk—so I bobbed out of reach, grabbed his fist as it went by my face, and twisted his arm.

He budged, cursed between his teeth, and I'll be damned if he didn't try to kick me. I put more strength into twisting his arm further, lifting him slightly. As his foot was about to come up off the step, he suddenly relented, and allowed me to lead him.

Behind me I heard Winston whispering to Alfilda to stay by Alwyn's door and make sure no one entered.

"Call me if anyone tries to force their way in," he told her before he came up the stairs behind me. It was easier going now that Sigvald was trundling along like a rag doll in my hands.

Winston walked past us, opened the door to his and Alfilda's room, and, with a sweep of his hand, gestured that I should enter first.

The blankets on the bed were flung aside and bunched up against the wall, the sheet curled so that it was clear the activity that had most recently taken place there had not been sleep. I suddenly realized how long it had been since I'd thought about Brigit. The mere thought sent a warm rush to my loins, and I hoped it wouldn't take us long to get the answers we needed.

Sigvald was trying to wrench himself free from my grasp, and once Winston let the door slide shut behind him, I didn't see any reason not to let him have his way. I let go of him and gave him a little push, which propelled him onto the bed.

"I'm going to . . ." Sigvald began.

"Answer a couple of questions, yes, you are," Winston agreed, wadding up a blanket behind the farmer so that he could sit more comfortably. "And the faster this goes, the sooner you can go lie down."

Sigvald belched and muttered, "What's going on?"

Apparently we'd piqued his interest now. Or maybe he was afraid of being found out?

I leaned against the wall, while Winston sat down on the foot of the bed.

"You haven't felt compelled to drink this much until now," Winston remarked.

Sigvald tried to look sternly at Winston, but made do with another burp as a response.

"Is there any specific reason that you decided to keep drinking until you were drunk this afternoon?" Winston asked. He glanced at me, and I made a face to show that I'd wondered the same thing. For a man who's not a soldier to kill another man is no small thing, and killers have been known before to try to drown their consciences and their crimes at the bottom of an ale keg.

"What the . . . what the hell else was I supposed to do?" He asked. His voice wasn't quite as slurred as it had been only a few moments before. "I mean . . . that shit reeve sure is keeping us here in his shit town for a shitting long time."

I've noticed before that drinking often shrinks men's vocabularies.

"So you were drinking because you were bored?" Winston asked.

"It's good ale," he said, tilting his head back and smiling.

"I asked why you were drinking."

"I heard you." Sigvald glanced slyly at Winston. "And I'm wondering why you're so interested in why I drink."

Was he suddenly sober now? I knew Winston had had the same thought when he responded, "When a man who has acted for several days like an honest man suddenly starts drinking non-stop, it arouses my curiosity."

"Well, you can just put your curiosity away again." Sigvald made to stand up. "I don't have to explain my actions to you or anyone else."

Sigvald was halfway to his feet when Winston commanded, "Halfdan!" Sigvald glared at me.

"I think you should sit back down again," I said, smiling amiably, "and answer my master's questions."

"Your master, right." Sigvald sank back down onto the bed, but whereas before he'd been leaning back on the wad of blankets, now he sat stiffly upright. "You're an odd thane to pick a man like him for a master."

I laughed and said, "It's fine as long as one does what he wants."

Sigvald peered at us slyly and asked, "Could I get a tankard of ale?"

I glanced at Winston, who didn't say anything, so I responded, "Once you've answered my master's questions, you can drink until dawn for all we care."

Sigvald sneered and retorted, "That's not what I want. I'm just thirsty."

I knew that thirst. It always came when the buzz was about to wear off, and it made your throat as dry as a sandy beach in the middle of summer.

Winston leaned forward slightly and asked, "So what have you been up to this afternoon, Sigvald?"

Like Winston, I understood that we had to start with today. Any discussion of Darwyn or Arnulf's murders would be pointless. There was a new crime, and that was what we had to focus on.

"Drinking, as you so cleverly surmised all on your own." Sigvald's answer came willingly enough.

"Alone?"

Sigvald shook his head almost arrogantly and said, "Only a pathetic man drinks alone."

"Kindly tell me then, who were you drinking with?" Winston asked politely.

"Well, first I ate with Sigurd—that's my son," he said with a smile, "but you already know that, don't you? Then he went off to the market with the two womenfolk, and I sat by myself for a while until Herward came in. We shared a few pitchers." He hiccupped. "And Bjarne was there, too. Or he came at some point," he was thinking out loud. "Yeah, he came. Along with Alwyn, who at first said no to a drink, but then he sat down anyway."

Winston and I listened in silence and then exchanged a glance.

"Did he say why he didn't want to drink?" Winston asked, sounding casual.

Sigvald furrowed his brow and asked, "Who? Oh, Alwyn? Yeah, he said he had some thinking to do." Sigvald chuckled deep in his throat. "And that's definitely not something Alwyn does very often."

"Did he say what about?"

"Nah. Then he sat down to drink with the rest of us after all." Sigvald looked up at Winston triumphantly.

"So you drank together, the four of you. What about your son and the women? They were in the tavern when Halfdan and I got here a little bit ago."

"They . . ." Sigvald thought it over for a while. "They came in at some point, I don't remember when. But they didn't drink anything."

"Did any of you leave the table?" Winston asked.

"Yeah, sure. We all went out for a piss, of course. And Alwyn has never been able to hold his liquor. I guess that's why he didn't want to sit with us to start with. He gets drunk so fast. So he went upstairs."

"And you?"

Sigvald snorted and said, "I stayed in the tavern."

"Did you go upstairs?"

"Nah. Well, yeah, I came up with Alwyn. He had a hard time with the stairs."

Winston gave me a look. As if I couldn't think for myself.

"And?" Winston prompted.

"And what?" Sigvald said. "Then I went back down again, after I got him onto his bed."

"Did he say anything?"

"Say anything? Yeah, he muttered something about how he'd figured it all out."

Winston straightened and then pressed, "And what was it that he'd figured out?"

"How the hell should I know?"

"And then you left him? Was he alright?"

"As alright as a drunk man can be."

"And you haven't seen him since?"

"Nope." Sigvald shook his head, then he stopped midmotion. "Well, actually . . . He was suddenly standing on the stairs."

"On the stairs? When, later?"

"Yeah, the rest of us had probably drunk another tankard or two," Sigvald said.

"And then he was standing on the stairs? Did he say anything?"

I leaned forward in anticipation.

"Yeah, he said that thing I told you about how he'd figured it all out."

"He said it again? Who was he talking to?"

Sigvald laughed. "No one. Everyone. He was drunk."

"But then he went back to his room?"

"Yeah, well, I helped him. We're sharing a room you know."

I looked at Winston, but he didn't notice because he was already asking his next question: "You went upstairs with him again?"

"Yeah, he was drunk, you know?"

"And then?"

"And then I came back down and kept drinking," Sigvald said.

"Did anyone else leave the table and go upstairs after that?"

"Yeah, Herward left for a while."

"Why?"

"How should I know? Maybe to get something. When he came back down, he'd grabbed his tunic. He was cold, he said."

The temperature had dropped with the rain, I remembered.

"And was he gone for a long time?" Winston asked.

"How should I know?" Sigvald asked again, shaking his head. "Listen, what's all this about?"

"Alwyn is dead," I said.

"Dead?" Sigvald stood up, but then sank back down again.

Neither Winston nor I had taken our eyes off his face. He looked appalled.

"Murdered," I continued.

Sigvald took a deep breath. "Stabbed?" he asked.

I nodded.

"And you think . . . that I . . ." Sigvald began.

"Was it you?" Winston asked without raising his voice.

"No, but . . ." Sigvald looked up. "That's why you wanted to know . . ."

I nodded again and asked, "Did Bjarne go upstairs at any point?"

Sigvald shook his head and sighed.

Winston suddenly asked, "Did you kill him together?" I stared speechlessly at Winston, but then understood what he was getting at. Unlike Sigvald, who stammered, "Together?"

Winston leaned forward and clarified, "You and Herward were coming down the stairs when we came into the tavern earlier."

"Oh, then." Sigvald flung up his hands in a gesture that suggested that wasn't important. "We were . . . We had decided not to drink more. But when we got halfway up the stairs, we decided there really wasn't much else to do."

"So you came back down again?" Winston didn't sound like he believed Sigvald any more than I did.

Sigvald nodded.

"So you . . ." I began, but was interrupted by a shout.

Winston was at the door in one step and flung it open. An angry male voice thundered at us, followed by Alfilda's protests.

I beat Winston to the door that concealed the body, getting there just as Herward pushed Alfilda aside and placed his hand on the latch.

32

was just going to . . ." Herward began, looking at Sigvald, who came down the stairs behind Winston. "Aren't you . . . ?"

I grabbed Herward's arm and pulled him away.

"You were just going to what?" Winston asked, holding Sigvald back with his arm.

Herward turned to Winston and said, "Talk to Sigvald."

"What about?" Winston's voice was gentle.

"That's no one else's business," Herward said, looking at Sigvald. "We were drinking together, right?"

"I've drunk my fill," Sigvald said, tugging uneasily on his beard. "Like I said."

"You did? Yeah, but then . . ." Herward began.

Winston nodded to me, and I opened the door. A faint whiff of ale mixed with the dull scent of blood hit us. Sigvald looked down at the floor, apparently not wanting to see. Herward stared first at me, then into the room. The fly buzzed over the dead man's chest.

"That . . ." Herward swallowed.

I pushed Herward through the doorway and followed him in. Just behind me was Sigvald, whom Winston pushed into the room.

"That is your neighbor." Winston's voice was anything but happy. "Murdered."

I didn't take my eyes off them. Sigvald gulped, glanced over at the body, and then turned to look at Herward. Herward had sucked his upper lip into his mouth and was biting it so hard that a drop of blood trickled out. He licked off the blood.

Their faces reflected fear, horror, revulsion, and uneasiness. I detected no trace of guilt.

Alfilda spoke. The four of us jumped since we'd all been focused on the body.

"People say the blood flows from a murdered man when his killer lays a hand on him. Would you both go place your hands on Alwyn?" she said.

That's an old wives' tale. I've seen plenty of men handling bodies they've killed without blood flowing. After a battle, a raid, or any kind of combat, only the survivors are left to clean up. Even I have carried the bodies of men I had just stuck my sword into a few moments before. Their bodies did nothing more than drag over the ground.

Still, I watched the two farmers in anticipation.

Sigvald clenched his teeth and stared at the air above the dead man as he stepped over to him. He put his hand on the corpse's chest so quickly that it was as if it didn't happen and then stepped back again.

Winston gave Herward a look of encouragement. Herward cleared his throat, the spit rumbling deep in his chest, and then he too walked over to the body, put his hand on its chest, and then hurried back over to the door.

"Herward." Winston's voice stopped him in his tracks. "Alfilda is right that that's what people say. Is it true? Who knows. But I need to ask you a few questions."

"You?" Herward's voice was raspy, as if he were trying to suppress some emotion. Grief, anger, or indignation at being subjected to this?

"What business is the killing of our companion to you?" Herward asked.

"It is very much my business. Believe me, Alwyn was killed to shut his mouth about what he knew, which is why the other two men were killed. And I promised to solve those murders, so this one has also fallen into my lap."

Herward looked at Winston expectantly. Winston paused for a moment and then continued, "Did you kill Alwyn?"

Herward looked over at Sigvald and said, "No."

"Do you know who killed him?"

He shook his head. The two farmers looked at each other.

"You came upstairs while you guys were downstairs drinking. Why?"

Herward seemed not to have heard him. He was staring at Sigvald. After a moment he looked back over at Winston and said, "What did you say?"

"When you were drinking, you came upstairs. Why?"

"Why?" Herward didn't seem to understand the question, and then in a voice that sounded choked up said, "I was cold. I came to get my tunic."

"From your room?"

Herward nodded.

"And you didn't come to this room?"

"Why would I do that?"

The answer to that question was so obvious that surely he must see it. Winston didn't even bother to respond, but made do with looking from Herward to Sigvald. Herward stood in the doorway, his legs set wide apart, his face white with anger. Sigvald stood between the body and Herward, and looked just as pale as his companion.

Winston said, "You can both go."

They left without looking at each other, and walked shoulder to shoulder down the stairs.

"Of course they're lying, one or both of them," Winston said, setting down his tankard.

Some time had passed since the farmers had been allowed to leave the dead man's room.

First I'd been sent down to get Willibrord, who looked fearfully at the body and then told us, shivering, that this market was the worst he remembered. It was bad enough that one of his guests had been murdered, but because the murder had taken place in the inn itself, he was afraid clients would stream away from him like water through a sluice.

"Or flock here," I suggested. "It won't take long before this will be just a good story that will draw people in."

The look the innkeeper gave me showed that he did not share my opinion.

It took a while to get the body carried out, after which we had to wait for the messenger who'd been dispatched to Turstan. The messenger returned later with word that the reeve would come see us in person or send his man. Until then, we were told, we mustn't leave town.

It wasn't until all this was done that we were finally able to leave the inn and find somewhere we could talk undisturbed. That place was an ale tent with its trestle tables set up on the grass and spaced apart nicely. There were two tables between the next closest patrons and us.

I liked this tent for another reason. It was right across from Brigit's husband's stall, so from my seat I had a view of her as she served their customers—virtuous as usual. Only once did she glance in my direction. I had made sure to speak loudly as we walked into the tent, and although I was engrossed in our conversation, I was still annoyed that she didn't seem to have noticed me.

"How likely is it that they went in on the killings together?" Alfilda wondered.

I shrugged. "Not very. It's hard to see a motive for it. But that doesn't mean that they're not lying for each other. Neighbors are like that. They stick together like pea straw against outsiders. Anyway"—I drank another gulp of ale—"that was brilliant, that stuff about bodies bleeding."

She chuckled and said, "I had hoped it would work out differently."

"Whichever one of them is the murderer wouldn't be afraid of a body," Winston said, tugging on his nose. "And you're right. I don't think they did it together. It was one of them. I have no doubt about that. But which?"

"I suppose we'd better start by asking why?" I suggested.

"Money," Alfilda and Winston said simultaneously.

I nodded in agreement. Arnulf's love of silver was all we had to go on. "A neighbor who owed Arnulf money?"

"Yes," Winston said eagerly. "A debt that for some reason or other suddenly became a burden when they got to town."

"After the Hundred Court was over with," Alfilda said.

We both stared at her.

"Say that again, would you?" Winston's voice was deep with surprise.

"Darwyn wasn't killed until the court session was over with." Alfilda looked from Winston's face to mine and then continued haltingly. "We thought it was because of the court's decision, that Darwyn was killed as revenge, but that wasn't it at all."

I thought I saw what she was getting at.

Winston continued, "That womanizing lad was killed in the hope of achieving revenge against Arnulf."

"Exactly." Alfilda's voice was shrill with excitement. She cleared her throat and proceeded in a more normal voice. "The murderer figured Delwyn would assume that Arnulf had killed his son."

"And Delwyn did," I pointed out.

"True," Alfilda said, "but what the murderer didn't count on was that we would be there when Delwyn came rushing at Arnulf to take his revenge. You"—she gestured at Winston—"prevented Delwyn from killing Arnulf in revenge and then you convinced Delwyn that Arnulf couldn't have been the murderer."

An involuntary whistle escaped me.

"The killer must have hated you right then, Winston," I said. "But we're forgetting one thing."

They raised their eyebrows at me.

"The farmers said they were together."

Winston laughed and said, "Didn't you just point out that neighbors stick together like pea straw? And especially against a thane."

"So they knew the whole time which of them was the murderer?" I asked.

"Not necessarily," Winston said. "They said they were together to help Arnulf. And maybe they weren't even lying. Maybe they *were* together in the sense that most of them had stayed in the same spot together most of the time. But men need to piss; sometimes one lingers at a market stall longer than his pals, or follows a shapely backside through the crowd for a little while. Not long enough for it to be conspicuous, but definitely long enough to stab a man to death."

"So they're strolling around the marketplace," I said. "One of them knows he has to do Arnulf in, and then happens to run into Darwyn."

Alfilda interrupted me eagerly, "And voilà, the idea is born."

"Exactly," I said, just as excited. "He pulls Darwyn into a storeroom, stabs him to death, and is back out with his companions before they notice he's gone."

"You're right," Winston said. "Now there's only one question left. Which one of them?"

We looked at one another.

"Sigvald," I said hesitantly. "He knew Gertrude was going to give Rowena to Sigurd if Arnulf died. He must also have known that after the court's decision, Arnulf wanted to take revenge by refusing to allow the two to be together. Irrational, but we know that's how it was. A farmer who's had a plump inheritance for his son waved in front of his nose doesn't look kindly on that promise being broken. With Arnulf out of the way, the situation suddenly improved."

"And," Winston said hesitantly, "in my opinion Sigvald is both shrewd and cold-blooded. He would know to seize an opportunity like the one that turned up when he ran into Darwyn."

Alfilda had been listening quietly. Now she leaned forward and said, "Do you remember the morning before the court session? We were eating our porridge for breakfast and Arnulf said . . ." She was struggling to remember. "He said, *A good day begins with a good meal.*"

"And then he followed with, *It will look lighter for us this evening than yesterday,*" I continued as I recalled his words.

"Exactly," Alfilda said. "When I think back on it, I realize Arnulf was talking to Herward specifically, and not to everyone there."

"But why would Herward's evening be lighter just because Arnulf won his court case?" I wanted to know.

"Because we know something else about Arnulf, besides just that he was avaricious," Alfilda said.

Winston suddenly nodded vigorously and blurted out, "He got so friendly when he was right."

"Exactly," Alfilda said. "Suppose Herward owed him money. And maybe Arnulf promised to forgive the debt if he won his case."

"No," I shook my head at her. "*When,* not *if.* Arnulf was sure he was going to win. That's why he reacted so strongly when it didn't happen. Ah," I smacked my forehead. "Arnulf said, *No pact or agreement can persist when the law permits this.* I used that against Sigurd, but he wasn't the only one who understood what Arnulf was saying."

I reached over and took Alfilda's hand. She looked at me in surprise.

"I think you're right," I said.

Winston gave me a look of approval and then said, "But the proof. Both Sigvald and Herward have enough friends here in town to swear themselves free. We lack proof."

"That will be hard with regard to Sigvald," I admitted, "since I'm just guessing. And the same is true of Herward. Gertrude doesn't know anything about Arnulf's business dealings—that information went to the grave with him."

"Well, not necessarily," Alfilda said. "A man like Arnulf didn't necessarily trust men at their word. What if he wrote his debtors down? Would he have come to town without bringing that list? I think it's worth going through his effects. Does Gertrude have them?"

I nodded.

Winston stood up and said, "You're right. It's worth a try. If it works, we have our murderer."

"And if it doesn't work?" I asked, getting to my feet as well.

"Then we'll have to try to lure one of them into a trap. But let's check if Arnulf had a list of debtors first."

I let them go ahead and then strolled over to the woolen goods stall on my way out. Brigit stood with her eyes downcast as I leaned in toward her.

"Expect me tonight," I said.

"But . . ." she didn't continue because her husband had turned toward us.

"Tonight," I repeated and hurried after my master and his lady friend.

33

hen we got back to the tavern, there was no trace of anyone from the village, so it took a while to track down Gertrude. Willibrord told us the three farmers had left the tavern just after us, and that the women and Sigurd had stuck around briefly before they went out as well.

This news about the farmers made us discuss whether there was a risk that they might run off. Winston didn't think so. If only one of them was guilty, he wouldn't dare reveal himself, and if he somehow did anyway, the others would keep him here.

"Why would they?" I protested.

"They're farmers, up against a powerful thane and the reeve. If they let a neighbor sneak off after he killed the thane's son and clearly broke the reeve's orders, they would certainly feel the weight of the noblemen's revenge."

I wasn't convinced. I was about to head out to look for Gertrude, in the hopes that she would let us look through Arnulf's effects, when Winston agreed with my suggestion to send one of the tavern's slaves to Stigand with news of the situation. Stigand was a man of action, and as soon as he realized who the message was from, I was confident he would send word to the guards at the town gates that they should keep an eye out and prevent any of the farmers from leaving town.

We decided Winston and Alfilda would stay at the inn to catch Gertrude if she turned up, while I took a turn through the market. I popped back into the tavern three times, since all of us wanted to be there when we finally talked to the widow. On each occasion, Winston looked up from the table right across from the door where he and Alfilda were sitting and shook his head.

I was on my fourth round of the market and coming down a narrow lane behind the wool merchant's stall when I allowed myself to take a brief rest, since the spot permitted an excellent view of Brigit's alluring rump.

A merchant with at least six boxes balanced on his head was trying to squeeze by me. His arms stretched upward as he strained to hold his swaying boxes in place. I took a step back to make room for him.

Someone behind me exclaimed in warning, but it was too late because I'd already stepped on his or her foot. That person turned out to be Gertrude, who eyed me reproachfully, and I hurriedly apologized for the pain I'd caused her.

"But you're just the person I've been looking for, Gertrude. My master is waiting for us back at the inn."

Women are funny. Most of the women I've encountered are unlike men. If you give a man a piece of information—let alone an order—most men will simply accept it without wanting to know why. Women on the other hand . . . I can't even count the number of times I've had to convince a woman to obey me, when a man would have just said "alright" and done whatever I'd said. In this regard, Gertrude was more like a man than a woman. She simply nodded, asked me to lead the way, and then calmly walked back to the inn with me.

This was not so much the case with Rowena, who followed in her lady's wake, hand in hand with Sigurd. Sigurd didn't say anything. In fact, he looked as though the world could demand anything it wanted of him as long as he could obey the orders without letting go of his girlfriend's hand. Rowena, on the other hand, began a barrage of questions: "What happened? Did you find anything out? Do you know who the murderer is?"

The wench peppered me with these questions and more. Relieved to have found Gertrude, I brushed all the questions aside as I led them toward the inn, where Winston and Alfilda got up the instant they saw us.

Winston politely asked Gertrude to follow him and Alfilda upstairs, and she immediately complied. Rowena apparently thought the request pertained to her as well, and since Winston made no move to stop her or Sigurd, I let them go ahead of me. Thus Rowena's bottom was right in front of my eyes as I climbed the stairs, and I was able to determine that its curves were every bit as nice as Brigit's.

Winston stopped in the hallway in front of the door to Gertrude's room and quietly explained to Gertrude what he wanted.

"We're certain that the murderer is one of two people. If among Arnulf's effects you can find some kind of account of who owed him money, we might be able to solve the case. Would you help us?"

The widow nodded and held her hand up to shush Rowena, who wanted to know immediately who the two men were.

"Listen, my child," Gertrude told her. "You and I can both figure out they're men from the village, otherwise my husband wouldn't have recorded anything about them. Of course you're afraid one of them is your future father-in-law, but I honestly don't care. For me it's a question of getting this business resolved so we can go home and get going on everything that's waiting there."

A wise woman. Amazingly enough, Rowena didn't say anything, but what struck me most was that Sigurd didn't react at all to the notion that his father might be a murderer. Apparently he was still satisfied just to be able to hold Rowena's hand. There you see what being in love can do to a man.

The women's room wasn't large. Actually, it was so small that Winston chose to step aside and let Gertrude go in while he signaled to the rest of us with a hand gesture that we should wait outside.

I stared past Alfilda's shoulder at the widow, who leaned over and fished around under the bed. A moment later she stood up with a leather pouch in her hand.

She loosened the drawstring that held it closed and dumped the contents onto the bed. We all instinctively craned our necks and followed her hand excitedly as she picked through the things she'd dumped out: a narrow ingot that gleamed of silver, four gold coins, two silver armbands, and a flat wooden disk.

Winston exhaled a sigh, cocked his head at Gertrude, and when she nodded, held out his hand for the disk.

The light in the hallway where we were standing wasn't good enough, so Winston had to push his way past Gertrude to the little round window at the far side of the tiny bedroom.

We watched him in silence as his fingers followed the marks carved in the wood. Finally he looked up and summoned me over to him with a bent finger. I obeyed, watching wide-eyed as he handed me the disk.

Though I hadn't mastered the art of reading and Winston knew as much, I let my eyes scan the wood and laughed to myself.

Of course Arnulf hadn't learned any of those odd letters that Winston and other schooled people use either. Runes, on the other hand, he was familiar with, and like me he could both carve them and read them.

As we stepped back into the tavern, I couldn't help but gasp involuntarily because just as we set our feet on the floor, the door opened and the three farmers walked in. I grinned at Winston and he responded with a shrug of his shoulders, because he didn't believe any more than I did in miracles that made men appear just when it suited us best.

They noticed our serious expressions as we approached them.

"You have news?" Sigvald asked.

Winston said, "Yes. Shall we have a seat?"

He had Gertrude and the young lovers sit all the way against the wall, Bjarne next to them, and Alfilda at the end of the table. He sat down at the other end and gestured that Herward and Sigvald should sit down on the bench on the long side of the table, which they did, both with uneasy glances at me when I didn't sit down but instead leaned against a pillar just behind them.

Willibrord rushed over and when Winston requested tankards of ale for everyone, our host made a clicking noise to a slave wench that she should bring the first few and he would bring the rest as soon as he'd filled them.

Winston raised his tankard, drank, and then set it down. None of the farmers drank.

"Three hundred shillings. More than your farm is worth, I would imagine." Winston dropped the words onto the table, but all of us who'd been up in the women's room a minute ago knew whom he was talking to.

Sigvald apparently also figured it out, because he turned toward Herward.

Herward licked his lips.

"Had Arnulf promised to forgive your debt if he won the court case?" Winston asked, looking right into Herward's eyes. "Even though," he continued, "it wasn't like him to forgive such a large sum. Surely he would sooner have offered you some sort of peaceful arrangement."

Herward didn't say anything. His eyes were twitching.

"Did the sheep deal fall through?" Winston asked. "And yet. Only an idiot would lose three hundred shillings on a sheep deal."

Sigvald turned to Herward and said, "You've never been a good farmer."

"No, we heard that while we were waiting for you back in the village," Winston said. "So you put money into both farming and sheep trading?"

Herward tried to stand up from the bench, but I stepped forward and placed my hand on his shoulder.

"I'm sorry," he said. It took a couple of heartbeats before I realized that he was speaking to Gertrude.

"He should have kept his word," Herward muttered.

"So I was right," Winston said. "You agreed to an amicable solution?"

Herward suddenly seemed drained of his strength. His body slumped, and even his tousled hair looked thinner than before.

"I've been losing money for years. Arnulf was willing to loan me money and, without my realizing it, my debt grew out of control. Last winter he laid it out for me, how much I owed him. I couldn't even make reasonable installment payments. I had to transfer my farm to him. And then the rape . . ." He looked at Rowena, who looked back without blinking. "The court case was supposed to . . . Well, you knew him. He was almost giddy at the thought of winning against a nobleman. So he promised me I could stay on the farm if he won . . . no, *when* he won . . . and pay off the debt in installments."

"A promise that he took back after the court decision?" Winston said.

Herward nodded.

Winston continued. "And then you were powerless, so impotent that you seized the opportunity when you ran into Darwyn."

"I didn't plan it. It just happened," Herward said, nodding again.

"But then I prevented Delwyn from killing Arnulf and you were forced to do it yourself."

Another nod.

"And then Alwyn came to see you?"

Herward shook his head and said, "No, but he knew of my distress. One time when I was drunk, I confided in him." A tear ran down Herward's cheek, paving the way for more, which wet his beard. "He was a man of his word, Alwyn, and he didn't tell anyone. But then—"

"Then suddenly he was standing here in the tavern, claiming he'd figured the whole thing out," Winston summarized and drank a swig of ale.

We were all staring at Herward, who was on the verge of sobbing outright.

"He was a good man," Herward said.

Unlike Arnulf, I understood him to mean. The murderer had not shed any tears at the loss of that skinflint Arnulf.

A deafening silence prevailed around the table. Rowena squeezed Sigurd's hand, Gertrude cried softly to herself, and Bjarne glanced at Sigvald, who was sitting very still.

"What are you going to do . . . to me?" Herward asked feebly.

"I suppose I'll have to . . ." Winston began, but was interrupted by the sound of the door. We all turned and saw Delwyn striding across the floor, his footsteps heavy. He was followed by three spearmen.

"The reeve tells me you've had the gates sealed." Delwyn eyed Winston coolly.

"That's not entirely correct. I . . ." Winston didn't get any further than that.

Delwyn's eyes were glued to the sobbing Herward.

"Him?" the thane asked.

We were all silent. The farmer crying was the only sound.

Delwyn leaned toward the Saxon farmer and growled, "You murdered my son?"

Herward collapsed, sinking to his knees on the floor like an empty bladder, where he clasped the thane's calves, pleading, "I'm sorry, I'm sorry."

I heard the door open again and turned to look in spite of the drama unfolding before me. Stigand stood in the doorway.

Delwyn kicked at Herward, who continued to cling to his legs, and when Delwyn couldn't free himself, he reached down and grabbed the farmer's shoulder. He pulled him to his feet and shoved him forcefully toward the door.

"Out!" he yelled.

Herward yammered and stretched out his hands to us at the table. No one moved.

Stigand stepped aside to make way for the thane's spearmen. They went out, and then another shove sent the murderer out the door. Breathing heavily, Delwyn strode after him, followed by the rest of us. Gertrude tried to hold Rowena back, but the girl shook her mistress's hand off and pulled her boyfriend outside with her. Alfilda squeezed Winston's hand, and I walked out with Sigvald. Only Bjarne remained seated at the table, I noted.

By the time I made it outside, Herward was crawling away from Delwyn, sobbing. Delwyn ordered his men forward with a yell.

I turned to Stigand and said, "Doesn't the reeve have anything to say about this?"

Stigand gave me a gruff smile and replied, "If I understand things correctly, that man is the murderer?"

I nodded.

"And Delwyn is entitled to take revenge on him for murdering his son?" Stigand said.

I nodded again. Stigand's only response was a raised eyebrow.

The men had gotten Herward to his feet and turned him to face the thane. Delwyn drew his sword and was striding toward the farmer with his weapon drawn. With a howl, the Saxon farmer freed himself from the men's grasp, turned and staggered away, wracked with sobs, but was stopped by the circle of chattering, curious onlookers who had flocked around at the first sign that something was going on.

While Herward searched in vain for an opening in the crowd that he could slip away through, Delwyn stood, legs wide apart, weighing his sword in his hand.

"Turn around and meet your destiny," Delwyn said, his voice slicing through the murmur of the onlookers.

Herward screamed and tried to push his way into the crowd at the closest point. When he couldn't manage to force his way through, he turned around and ran sobbing around the perimeter of the circle.

Delwyn grimly watched Herward's attempt to get away, which was foiled by the ring of onlookers. Then he resheathed his sword and held out his hand to one of his spearmen, who handed him his spear. He weighed the spear in his hand, peered at Herward's back, and then let the weapon fly. It took less than a heartbeat from when it left his grasp until it skewered Herward's back.

Herward fell flat on his face, howling in pain, and kicking at the ground with his feet. His body shuddered. His muscles tensed in pain and then relaxed as he died with the sudden stench of shit.

By then, Thane Delwyn had already turned and left.

34

The message arrived from Delwyn just as we sat down to dinner. Winston, Alfilda, and I were on our own. None of the others were in the tavern. Gertrude had been up in her room since we'd returned to the inn, and Rowena was with her. Sigurd had reluctantly consented to go with his father to see the reeve.

Sigvald had wanted Turstan's word that they could leave Thetford. Of course he realized as much as we did that the reeve's orders for the farmers not to exit the gates could no longer apply. Still he insisted on obtaining permission to leave from Turstan's own mouth so that—as he put it—he wouldn't be guilty of having disobeyed an order.

It had been seen before, he claimed. We nodded in confirmation that since farmers did indeed have to pay a price for not having secured a nobleman's explicit permission, it was wise to obtain the reeve's express consent in advance.

Bjarne had not come outside with us when we followed the revenge-hungry Delwyn, but we found him at the door when we returned to the tavern after Herward was killed.

Bjarne walked over to his dead neighbor's body in silence. The body lay alone on the ground now that the onlookers had drifted off and Delwyn's spearmen had left with their master. Bjarne bent over the body, briefly placed his hand on Herward's shoulder, and then stood back up.

From the doorway I had watched him walk over to Stigand, ask him a question, and then look around as Stigand nodded. Bjarne spotted three shabbily dressed men of the type that can be found in any town, who get by on whatever work is available, and summoned them over. A coin wandered from his hand to one of theirs, after which they picked up Herward's body and carried him off, followed by Bjarne, who didn't look back.

After that, I had sat alone over a tankard of ale, wondering how early Brigit would leave her husband's market stall and return to her room. I decided probably not until after dinner, so I welcomed Winston and Alfilda when they joined me. They'd been up in their room since we came back inside and now wanted something to eat, which suited me just fine since I hadn't eaten anything since the bread and pork I'd had with Alwyn.

"We'll move on tomorrow," Winston said, accepting a clay bowl of peas and pork from Willibrord, who nodded at the information.

I had asked for cabbage and pork and was enticed by the aroma that rose from the bowl placed in front of me.

"And what about Cnut's job?" I asked.

"That's what sends us on," Winston grumbled, wiping grease from the corners of his mouth. "We were sent to Saint Edmund's Town, I'm sure you remember. That's where our assignment is. The good coin makers gave me quite a bit of information, and I really think they're well informed enough that there's nothing more for us to obtain here in Thetford. But you know how a monastery buzzes with rumors. So let's head to Edmund's Town and keep our ears open."

He stuck a spoonful of peas in his mouth, chewed, and swallowed.

"And to be completely honest," Winston added, "I need to get to work again. Don't forget that our cover story is that I'm offering the monks my artistic services."

Alfilda, who was eating salt cod and stewed broad beans, looked up.

"I suppose it's also about time you find yourself something to do after leaving Halfdan and me to do all the murder investigation work," she said, turning to smile at me. "Now it's our turn to loaf around."

I could see that Winston was about to snap at her, but since his own girlfriend had said it and not me, he kept chewing in silence.

I pushed my bowl away, belched behind my hand, and watched the door open, revealing a well-dressed man who held himself like a soldier although he wasn't carrying any type of weapon. His hair was freshly washed and tied around the forehead with a blue band. His shirt was of fine linen and his wool breeches were wrapped with wide leather bands. A freeman employed by some nobleman, I thought, wondering whether I ought to request another tankard of ale.

The man scanned the tavern quickly and lit up when he spotted us.

"Winston the Illuminator?" He bowed briefly to my master, who nodded.

"I'm Toste, Thane Delwyn's stableman." His voice was courteous and he was speaking in Danish.

It did not surprise me that Delwyn was powerful enough to have a stableman to tend to his horses and other equipment.

Winston politely invited Toste to have a seat, which the stableman just as courteously declined.

"My master asks you to accept his gratitude." For the first time Toste's eyes fell on me, after which they touched on Alfilda and then returned to me again. "He recalls that you, who must be Halfdan, left it up to your master to decide whether you were going to solve his son's murder." He looked back at Winston. "Therefore he has instructed me to give Winston your reward for completing the work."

Winston shook his head and said, "That's good of the thane, but there was never any discussion of our being paid for allowing justice to be done."

"My master knows that," Toste said with a nod of approval. "But his son now lies avenged in his grave, and it would poorly become a nobleman if he did not show his gratitude that his son doesn't need to wander around without rest, but can take his seat at the high table in Valhalla with the one-eyed one."

Toste must have sensed our surprise because he continued with a smile, "My master is as good a servant of the White Christ as anyone else, but prefers to believe that noblemen go to the high halls when their earthly life is over. The thought of wandering around for eternity in a garden doesn't please him, and he thinks there's a thing or two the church men have misunderstood."

Delwyn wasn't the only one who thought that way, I knew. I had encountered the idea before, that a man who died unavenged was doomed to wander without rest as a shadow of himself.

"Which is why Thane Delwyn asks you to accept this." Toste set a leather pouch in front of Winston, who regarded it with a furrowed brow.

I knew it was quite plausible that Winston would find a way to turn it down, and I was just about to reach my hand out to secure the pouch when Toste abruptly bid us farewell and left the tavern.

We sat in silence, staring at the pouch. Alfilda broke the silence and said, "There it is. We might insult the thane if we send it back."

"Do you think . . . ?" Winston began.

We both nodded, and he undid the ties and poured the contents onto the table. The silver coins rolled, clinking across the tabletop; at Winston's signal, I began to count them.

"Two hundred shillings," I announced after I'd finished. "A farmer's wergeld."

"How fitting," mumbled Winston, reaching out and dividing the coins into two piles. He pushed one over to Alfilda and one to me. "Split it. You say you're the ones who did the work."

We both protested, Alfilda a little more than me, but he wouldn't budge.

"When I do my illuminations for churches and monasteries, the wages go to me alone, so it is right and reasonable that this is yours."

He looked up as Sigvald and Sigurd sat down at the table without any ado.

"Did you accomplish what you wanted?" Winston asked.

"Yes," Sigvald said, looking with curiosity at the stacks of coins Alfilda and I were sweeping toward us.

"Will you pardon us?" Winston said to the farmers before glancing over at me. "Now that you have some company here, Alfilda and I are heading back up to our room. It's been a long and eventful day."

I stood up, smiled at Sigvald, and said, "I don't want to be impolite, but I'm actually meeting someone."

"So you're going to do some more skirt chasing, huh?" Winston teased.

"Well, there's chasing and then there's catching. Let's just say I won't be back until tomorrow morning."

35

A blue twilight had settled over the town and the market-place. I heard the murmur of voices from people in the tents and stalls who were trying to squeeze in a good deal on the market's final day. Many of the merchants had sold out, if not at deep discounts, then at least cheaply enough so that they wouldn't have to carry their wares back home again.

I had an idea. The coins were clinking in my pouch, and let it never be said of me that I don't know how to show a girl how much I esteem her. So I strolled past the wool stand, where I was able to confirm that Brigit was still helping her husband with his work, and roamed through the market looking for a silversmith looking to make a good deal.

The first two I found were no good. The silver at the first one didn't look pure enough, a suspicion I considered confirmed by the fact that the silversmith hadn't sold much. Maybe I wasn't the only one who suspected him of mixing too much copper into his silver?

The second refused to haggle for the few items he had left. He said he was going to sell them for his asking price, and if that didn't happen, there were so few items left that he could easily carry them back to his hometown of York.

But then luck was with me at a stand that was set off on its own a bit, behind a shoemaker's shop. I liked the jewelry that was out on the counter, and one piece in particular caught my eye. It was a pendant, composed of twisted silver wires curling under and over each other.

The silversmith, who saw me admiring the piece, told me it was an Irish piece he'd bought off a Viking, and then there was no doubt left in my mind. A piece of Irish jewelry had to be the right thing to give Brigit, and after a bit of haggling, the silversmith offered it to me for five shillings, which, he assured me, was less than the actual silver was even worth.

I sucked on my lips hesitantly and negotiated some more, responding that if he threw a chain in with it, I'd give him three and a half shillings.

We settled on four, and I hung the necklace around my neck, but tucked it inside my tunic.

The road to Brigit's building ran past the wool merchant's stall, and to my surprise—because darkness had fallen by now and there were no more customers in sight—Brigit was still with her husband.

So I sat down at an ale stand from where I had an unimpeded view of Brigit's stall, ordered a tankard of their best ale—I could afford to splurge tonight—and waited for her to go home.

It didn't happen.

My tankard was empty, and her husband had lain down in the cart behind the stand ages ago, but she didn't seem as if she was planning to leave. To the contrary, I was surprised when I saw her set out a couple of bales of wool and cover them with her cape. It looked like she was going to sleep there.

I got up and realized I was the last customer in the ale tent. As I emerged into the lane, I saw the marketplace was deserted apart

from a few merchants who were packing up their stands, presumably so that they could head out of town early and be on their way
before the roads were crowded.

I reached the wool merchant's stall, where Brigit was sprawled
on her woolen perch. She was lying there with her eyes open, and
I thought that she was waiting for me.

I was about to climb over the counter, but she stopped me.
Then she stood up silently and walked over to me. I reached my
hand out to her, but she didn't take it.

"What are you doing here?" I asked quietly, despite the anger
growing within me.

She glanced over her shoulder at the cart and said, "I'm in my
stall."

"We had a date."

"A date?" Her eyes shone in the gleam of the waning moon.

"Yes," I hissed. "We made it this afternoon, remember?"

"No," she said, surprised. "I don't recall any date, but I do
remember a man telling me to expect him. He didn't ask what I
wanted the way a person requesting a date would."

The devil with this girl! I felt my throat seize up in anger.
"Oh, bollocks . . ."

"No," she hissed. "I told you. There are plenty of young men
willing to make an attractive woman happy. I don't need to be
bossed around by someone like you."

"Oh for . . ." I grabbed at her irritably.

She evaded me.

"You should leave. Before my husband wakes up."

"Oh, your husband," I laughed. "What a threat."

"Leave, or I'll scream," she said, her voice cold. "The reeve's
guards patrol the marketplace."

I realized I'd lost. I had no desire whatsoever to fight whichever of Turstan's soldiers showed up. They'd just see things from her side: a virtuous merchant's wife who had seen her husband off to bed and was then assaulted by a strange man.

I snarled a farewell to her and stomped back down the lane.

I briefly considered seeking out a lady of the night, but put the thought out of my mind. It was Brigit I wanted, not some random, cheap tart. So I headed back to the inn, which fortunately wasn't locked although the tavern was deserted. Only Willibrord was in there, bossing a slave around to get the place cleaned up so that he could go to bed himself.

I bowed my head as a good-night, took a tallow candle from the counter, and headed upstairs. When I reached the door to my room, I pushed it open.

Someone cried out in fear. Puzzled, I stepped into the room and raised the candle. Its glow revealed two naked bodies in the bed Sigurd and I had been sharing.

Brigit was a beauty, but she had nothing on Rowena, who sat up, striving to cover her breasts, which jutted out at me girlishly and provocatively. Both she and the boy at her side were covered with the sweet sweat of lovemaking, and they both stared at me in speechless surprise.

"What in thunderation is going on in here?" I was in no mood to play nicey-nicey. "Not that I can't tell what's going on here!"

Sigurd wrapped the girl in the blanket, but quickly realized that in doing so he'd exposed his own half-erect penis and hurriedly covered that with his hand.

"But you said . . ." Sigurd began. He had to clear his throat before he was able to continue. "You said you wouldn't be back until early tomorrow."

I glared at him. Then I looked back at the girl, who was biting her lip and was so marvelous that I felt my own nether rod rising.

"Did I say that?" I grumbled. "If so, that information was for my master, not an invitation to defile my bed with illicit lovemaking."

Tears suddenly appeared in the wench's eyes, showing me how foolish I was being. Lord, they had only seized the opportunity when it arose and shouldn't have to pay for my having been treated poorly by Brigit.

The boy was already getting out of bed when I stopped him.

"Alright, listen, it's fine. You thought I'd be away all night, but I . . . my plans changed. You just stay here." I was reaching for the door, when a thought struck me. "You're going to get married, aren't you?"

"As soon as Arnulf is buried," Rowena said.

I reached under my tunic and removed the necklace, which I then handed to Rowena.

"Here, let this be my wedding present."

I closed the door behind me on their dumbfounded gratitude, which probably had more to do with my leaving them to finish their lovemaking than the gift itself, and trudged back down to the tavern. I told a stunned Willibrord that I was going to sleep on one of his tables and asked him to bring me a blanket.

About the Author

© Ilona Dreve

Bestselling Danish novelist Martin Jensen was born in 1946 and worked as a teacher and a headmaster in Sweden and Denmark before becoming a full-time writer in 1996. The author of twenty-one novels, he has been honored by the Danish Crime Academy twice and was awarded the Royal Library's Prize for his medieval novel *Soldiers' Whore*. He and his wife are botany enthusiasts who also enjoy bird-watching and gathering mushrooms.

About the Translator

Tara F. Chace has translated more than twenty novels from Norwegian, Swedish, and Danish. Her most recent translations include Martin Jensen's *The King's Hounds* and *Oathbreaker* (AmazonCrossing, 2013 and 2014), Sven Nordqvist's *Findus Disappears!* (NorthSouth, 2014), Jo Nesbø's *Doctor Proctor's Fart Powder* series (Aladdin, 2010–2013), Lene Kaaberbol and Agnete Friis's *Invisible Murder* (Soho Crime, 2012), and Johan Harstad's *172 Hours on the Moon* (Little, Brown Books for Young Readers, 2012).

An avid reader and language learner, Chace earned her PhD in Scandinavian languages and literature from the University of Washington in 2003. She enjoys translating books for adults and children. She lives in Seattle with her family and their black lab, Zephyr.